JARED LARSON

JAC JEMC
FALSE BINGO

Jac Jemc is the author of *The Grip of It*, a finalist for the Chicago Review of Books Award for Fiction and one of *Vulture*'s ten best thrillers of 2017; *A Different Bed Every Time*, one of Amazon's best story collections of 2014; and *My Only Wife*, a finalist for the 2013 PEN/Robert W. Bingham Prize for Debut Fiction and winner of the Paula Anderson Book Award. She teaches writing in Chicago.

FALSE BINGO

FALSE BINGO

STORIES

JAC JEMC

MCD x FSG Originals

Farrar, Straus and Giroux

New York

MCD × FSG Originals
Farrar, Straus and Giroux
120 Broadway, New York 10271

These stories previously appeared, in slightly different form, in the following publications: *Puerto del Sol* ("Gladness or Joy"), *Southwest Review* ("Delivery"), *Ninth Letter* ("Strange Loop"), *Los Angeles Review of Books* ("The Principal's Ashes"), *Tiny Crimes* ("Any Other"), *New South* ("Don't Let's"), *Spork* ("Get Back"), *Paper Darts* ("Pastoral"), *The Butter* ("The Halifax Slasher"), *Fanzine* ("Bull's-Eye"), *StoryQuarterly* ("Half Dollar"), *Funhouse* ("Manifest"), *Crazyhorse* ("Maulawiyah"), *The Masters Review* ("Hunt and Catch"), *Guernica* ("Trivial Pursuit"), and FSGOriginals.com ("Kudzu").

Library of Congress Cataloging-in-Publication Data
Names: Jemc, Jac, 1983– author.
Title: False bingo : stories / Jac Jemc.
Description: First edition. | New York : MCD × FSG Originals, Farrar, Straus and Giroux, 2019.
Identifiers: LCCN 2019014949 | ISBN 9780374538354 (pbk.)
Classification: LCC PS3610.E45 A6 2019 | DDC 813/.6—dc23
LC record available at https://lccn.loc.gov/2019014949

Designed by Richard Oriolo

Our books may be purchased in bulk for promotional, educational, or business use. Please contact your local bookseller or the Macmillan Corporate and Premium Sales Department at 1-800-221-7945, extension 5442, or by e-mail at MacmillanSpecialMarkets@macmillan.com.

www.fsgoriginals.com • www.fsgbooks.com
Follow us on Twitter, Facebook, and Instagram at @fsgoriginals

1   3   5   7   9   10   8   6   4   2

For my grandmothers,
Dorothy and Lorraine

Where all are guilty, no one is; confessions of collective guilt are the best possible safeguard against the discovery of culprits, and the very magnitude of the crime the best excuse for doing nothing.

—HANNAH ARENDT, "ON VIOLENCE"

CONTENTS

ANY OTHER

HE FOUND HER ALREADY SEATED AT THE COFFEE shop.

"It's so nice to finally meet you." He held out his hand.

Bethany paused before accepting.

"I'm Keith," he said once her fingers were wrapped in his, and laughed at himself. "Of course, you know that. I'm sorry. May I?" He gestured to the chair across from her.

Bethany nodded, wondered why he didn't get himself a cup of coffee first.

"No use in wasting time, so I'll just ask," he said. "Have you made a decision?"

Bethany responded honestly. She shook her head.

"Good, then I can still convince you." Keith scooted his chair forward. "I know it's a family heirloom, but if you keep it locked away in storage, what difference does it make if you technically own it or someone else does? If you sell it to me, you can visit it. I can loan it to you. We could even agree that you can buy it back at any time."

Bethany wondered why it mattered so much to him. That he wanted it so very badly made her want to refuse him the satisfaction. "How much are you willing to pay?" she asked.

Keith blinked rapidly. "Well, we discussed fifty thousand dollars."

Bethany frowned. She had learned to do this during negotiations of any kind.

Keith filled his lungs. "But I'm prepared to go up to seventy-five thousand dollars." He looked down at her coffee cup now, ready to wait for her response.

"Would you get me a refill?" she asked. She enjoyed this power. She held it tight.

Keith jumped up. "Of course." She could feel his relief at stepping away. He ushered her mug over to the counter and asked the barista for a cup of his own, as well. She watched him closely as he pulled out a few bills. She examined the repetitive wear of his wallet on his back pocket. She noticed the bevel of the outside heel of his shoes, evidence of uncorrected supination and thriftiness. The money he offered her could be better spent.

4

When Keith returned, he looked expectant, hopeful the delay might have delivered a verdict.

He sipped his coffee. "I'm happy to answer any questions." He smiled.

Bethany found the way he forced himself to keep his gaze on her willful. She respected his determination and broke eye contact herself to see his index finger fidget the cuticle of his thumb, torn raw and red.

"Or maybe I can ask you a question," Keith said. "What's holding you back? Why not sell it?" He lifted his mug to his lips again.

Something about this query settled it for Bethany. "I'm sorry," she said. "No deal."

Keith set his mug down a little too hard. Coffee rushed over the edge of the cup and ran down the tilt of the table into his lap. "Shoot," he said. He ran to retrieve some napkins, wiping first at the splash on his pants and then mopping at the edges of the mug on the table. Bethany didn't move or speak. When Keith finally resettled, he said, "Why?"

Bethany looked into Keith's eyes for the answer, but all she turned up was the realization that she didn't need to explain it to him. She felt her shoulders flinch, as if the decision mattered little to her, no possibility of reversing it.

"There's nothing I can do to convince you?"

She shook her head and tightened her lips.

Keith stood, a ball of wet napkins clenched in his fist. "Okay," he said. "You know where to find me if you change your mind." Blood swamped her heart. "Have a good afternoon, then." Keith turned away, but spun back again. "I don't have it, but if I'd offered a hundred thousand, would that have made a difference?" he asked.

"No," she said. She held out her hand, hoping to end the conversation as it had begun, before she remembered the wad of napkins. She placed her palm back on the table.

"Then why . . . All right. Thank you, Joanne." Adrenaline rushed behind the name *Joanne*, but Bethany maintained her composure. Keith walked away with purpose. He pulled open the door and Bethany watched through the window as he disappeared right and then crossed back left, changing his mind about where he was headed or unfamiliar with the neighborhood.

Bethany wondered what it was Keith had wanted. She wondered what Joanne had to give. She wondered why she felt like it was her place to decide for both of them, but it had all unfolded so easily. She took a last sip of her coffee and gathered her things.

A woman in a polished pantsuit walked through the door, her eyes looking for someone. She asked at the counter about the man whom she was supposed to meet.

Bethany let her fingers fall on the shoulder of the woman as lightly as possible and leaned in. "Joanne?" The woman's whole body pursed under Bethany's touch. "Keep it," she whispered.

DELIVERY

WHEN THE FIRST PRINTER SHOWED UP, WE AL-
most refused delivery, so certain were we it was a mistake.
We opened the box to find a receipt from the shopping channel that plainly displayed Mother's name. "I didn't order
this!" she exclaimed, and we believed her. She didn't even
know how to turn on the computer, so why would she order a
printer? In the payment field of the bill, we saw that the QVC
charge had been submitted through our cable provider. We
wound up our faces in confusion, ready to retape the box
shut, when we thought to check with Dad just in case.

. . .

Pausing at the bottom of the basement stairs, we said, "Dad, did you order this?"

The blank look in his eyes said a lot, but we read it as a distracter, not the answer itself. "I might have," he said, taking the receipt from us. "That's a good deal." He pointed at the old linoleum table, recently relegated to the basement because of its solid wood successor now looming in the kitchen. We placed the box on its surface.

When the video game system showed up the next week, we went to Dad first. "You ordered a Wii?" the two of us asked. He had been an early adopter of Atari back in the seventies, but he'd abstained from purchasing another system since then, sticking instead to his collection of board games and then moving on to *SimCity*, *Doom*, *Myst*, before settling into the mundane game suite included with most PCs. We did not think of him as a video game kind of guy. "A wee bit of what?" he said, laughing at his own dad joke.

"A Nintendo Wii," we said, and recognition blinked onto his face. He confirmed and went about plugging in wires and scanning through options on the screen, and for the next week we heard the sounds of synthetic bowling rumble in the basement below us, until the day we brought down another box, and saw that the system had been dismantled, its cords and plastic casings piled haphazardly back into the box in which it had been delivered. "Why did you take it down?" we asked, but he shrugged, eyeing the new box in our hands. We hadn't opened it this time. We recognized the name of the warehouse on the return label, and ushered it to him directly. "What's in this one?" we asked.

"Let's see," he said with a coy smile. When we lifted out the twenty-one-inch flat-screen, it didn't seem like an unreasonable purchase considering he'd set up the video game system on a tiny ten-inch box set.

"Will you set up the Wii again now?" we asked, but he went back to his computer without answering us. He had never been talkative, and we saw a lack of response as advice that we should do away with our own verbal excesses. We told ourselves to mind our own business, so he didn't have to. He had trained us well.

When the set of reading glasses showed up, he said they were a birthday gift for our mother and we wrote off the weak prescription and the fact that her birthday was still months away as sweet mistakes. When the laptop came, we considered how old his desktop computer was and how easy this would be to carry from room to room. When the flip cam arrived, his first grandson was about to be born to the sister who had moved away, and so we could understand that, too.

"You caught the shopping bug, huh?" we joked with him, and he'd smirk like he had a secret. In reality, we blamed the purchases on his boredom. Newly retired, at a loss for how to fill his time, he had developed an interest in electronics.

· · ·

In the beginning, Mother embraced his shopping. "Let him do what he wants," she said, recognizing that he'd worked long and hard on his end of their partnership, the breadwinning.

When it didn't stop after a few weeks, though, she saw her spending power threatened by his advancing proclivities. When coin sets started showing up with retail values listed high above their denomination, she asked him to explain what made them special. He turned away, as if he didn't owe her an explanation and she knew it. She had always been the shopper in the family, and for every one package delivered to him, three others waited on the front porch addressed to her: a new dust ruffle, a fresh white jean jacket, a glass seashell with a bronze mermaid perched on the edge—each item decorative rather than functional. She paid the ever-expanding cable bill each month with a wince, but penned the check to Mastercard with a righteously smooth hand.

The shape of the next box seemed familiar, but there had been so many boxes, who could remember for sure? When he opened it up, we said, "Another printer?" It was a duplicate of the one he'd purchased just weeks before. "It must be a mistake," we said. "We'll send it back."

"No," he said, "I ordered it. Don't take it away."

"Why would you order a second, identical printer?" we asked.

"None of your business," he said.

"What will you do with it?" we persisted, but he turned back to his game of *Spider Solitaire* on the old desktop computer, the laptop still untouched in its box.

When the second video game system appeared, we considered not showing it to him at all. "Did you order a second Wii?" we asked from the top of the stairs.

"What?" he called.

"There's another Nintendo Wii here," we said, but he didn't answer, and one of us was tasked with taking it back to the post office.

When the third Wii showed up, we grew concerned. We called QVC and while we were on hold Dad walked through the kitchen, saw the open box, and carried it downstairs without comment. The customer service representative came back on the line and said each system had been ordered through the cable box on different dates. It was as simple as pressing some buttons. We asked the cable company to disable this feature, and waited for Dad to realize and complain, but he never mentioned it.

"Is he getting drunk and forgetting?" we asked Mom, but we found no empty liquor bottles in the trash cans. The beer fridge remained stocked with the same twelve-pack of lager that tasted flat and flavorless when we poured them into pint glasses for visitors.

It was around this time that he started disappearing behind the wood panels in the walls of the basement. He pitched out our old Fisher-Price playhouses and trash bags full of stuffed animals, all frosted with mold and the singed yellow of cigarette smoke. We balked, but we also knew we were too old to put up a fight.

We had a yard sale, sure someone would love the three-legged cat toy or the Lego sets with pieces missing, but the only profit we turned was from the Country Time lemon-ade we portioned out into Dixie cups, the pine cones we idly plucked from beneath the jagged skirt of our yard's only shade, and the complete collection of our childhood ceram-ics sold to a suspicious young man with a neck tattoo who we speculated might take a sledgehammer to them on YouTube.

We dropped the rest off at the Goodwill, but we noted the look on the face of the volunteer taking the donation, resigned to hauling the bags out of sight until our car pulled away, and then pitching them into the dumpster out back, an act of generosity we felt guilty to require of him.

After the secret storage compartments were emptied out, we found Dad setting up facsimiles of the basement in the cramped closets behind the wall panels. The first duplicate bore a modest resemblance to the rest of the basement: A rolling filing cabinet held a TV and the third Wii Dad had spirited away. A small TV tray table hosted the coins of which he'd purchased two sets. A canvas director's chair stood in for his recliner. He'd found older versions of our school pictures that hung on the walls beside his desk, and tacked those into the drywall. The light of the closet's single bulb burned warmer than the cold fluorescent fixture installed in the main room.

In the second compartment, the old cathode TV and a fourth Wii we hadn't even seen arrive sat propped on an old fruit crate in front of a dented metal folding chair. On a cardboard box turned on its end, a single Wisconsin quarter, the third he'd purchased, shined with its erroneous extra leaf stamped onto the tails side. Instead of photos on the walls, he'd sketched our likeness onto pages of the free notepads he'd accumulated from banks and auto repair shops—our faces misshapen, optimistic, unaware of our forced endorsement.

"You might be losing it," we joked, but alone, in our rooms, we thought of the way he'd imposed our faces on the paper, about what possessed him.

One summer afternoon, checking our email on his old desktop machine, we noticed his checkbook left out beside the computer, flipped open to a random page. We eyed the numbers casually, surprised to see as much money at the ready as there was, but then our eyes caught: two checks to the gas company for the same amount, written a day apart. We paged down and saw three debits to cover the property taxes and four equal payments made in the same day for our technologically spiked electricity.

We were afraid of embarrassing Dad, and so we took the

checkbook quietly up to Mother, while Dad dozed in the family room.

"What's the meaning of this?" she hollered, waving the register in Dad's face. "Why on earth are you paying bills more than once? Quit it, would you?"

We offered to write the checks for a while. It would be good practice for us before we went away to school. Mother could even proofread our work, but she waved us off.

"You're going soft in retirement," Mom said to Dad. "You need to keep better track of this stuff."

We were starting to get the idea that maybe he wasn't aware of what he was doing, but our mother thought he was doing it on purpose, running down their accounts to teach her a lesson about her own spending.

When fall came, we'd walk into the room and Dad would say, "Where have you been?"

We'd say we'd been to the store or for a walk or just reading a book in the other room.

"I haven't seen you all morning," he'd say, and we'd insist we'd eaten breakfast together.

"I didn't have breakfast," he'd say, and we'd remind him of the bagel with cream cheese and hard-boiled egg. "Must have been your other dad." That grin would show up and he'd stop talking.

We hoped he was kidding, but went down to the hidden

passages in the basement to look for a second or third dad all the same, just to be sure.

One afternoon he went out and didn't come home until the next morning. When he did reappear—his shirt rumpled and his face unshaven—he shook out a ragged cough and lay down. A deep scrape dented the driver's side of his car. "Where were you?" we asked.

"What do you mean? I was at home," he said, appending, "with my first wife." Of course, our mother was his first and only wife. This was his favorite joke, but today we paused before laughing.

As quickly as he multiplied, though, he divided. We asked him to walk to the ice-cream parlor, just four blocks away, but when we got halfway down our street, he insisted we turn back, out of breath, weak, unable to go any farther.

At restaurants, rather than ordering for himself, he looked at our mother with confusion and trust in his eyes, and told her to pick what he might like.

When we got in the car to head to his brother's house, he asked us which way to turn.

We realized that what had looked like an expansion was in fact a breaking down. What we'd ignored in increments had grown too large to control.

· · ·

When the doctor saw him, he pitied the poor care Dad had taken of himself, but it was us who had not been mindful. It was us who had let him go.

We hid the keys to the car, and eventually Dad stopped asking for them. We wrapped up old coins and pretended they were being delivered anew, and Dad delighted in them all the same. Once the utility bills had caught up with the credits on the accounts, Mom started paying them herself.

In the basement, while Dad watched reruns, we tried our hand at his favorite computer game, *Spider Solitaire*. We assembled the two decks of cards in order as best we could, but the blind stack wouldn't reveal what we needed to run all the cards off the table, and so we took our chances again and again.

Finally, we uncovered the card we needed, and the light stuttered from the screen as the cards danced around the virtual green-felt tabletop in victory.

From behind the wall panels hiding the replicas of the basement, we heard two more TVs playing the same channel displayed beside us, the sound of one falling just after the other, like sloppy dominoes. We heard Dad laugh and then we heard Dad laugh and then we heard Dad laugh.

STRANGE LOOP

JOHN SLIT THE SQUIRREL DOWN THE BELLY. HE pulled out the stuffed sausage of inner flesh. It was rare he saw blood leak onto the table, so precise were his shushing slides of the blade. When he was working like this the time went powdery. He rejoiced in the distracted exactitude.

John was a frame of madly hung trouble, but he had found a hobby that suited him. Hypnotized by the ziplocking of animal skins around wood wool forms, he created cradles for everlasting souls. He tendered their permutations with abandon. He doubled the undone.

He cringed at the idea of fauna allowed to empty by time and science. He filled the dark corners of these dancing beasts. His hands remembered the weight of each animal as he lifted it onto the table for the first time. He could lock in to that perfect moment of communion. More than the death boarded up within each creature's skin, he felt a vacated life.

John walked to the chapel alone in the mornings to pray and give thanks. He loved the moment the sunrise tipped through the windows onto his face, like an answer. He looked forward to this private stretch of time, to this unbroken focus.

John was thankful for having been restored to usefulness in the open world, free of the sparse room he'd inhabited for the past eight years, free of the aggression of the other inmates, free to season his food to his liking. It was true he could feel eyes on him when he visited the grocery store or bank, which made him wonder if people knew. But he did his best to soldier on. He made children invisible to him and pretended women didn't exist. Even despite the lining of sorrowful repentance, the liberty washed over him regularly, reminding him of relief and regret at once.

· · ·

John enjoyed hollowing snakes the most. He understood the symbolism: temptation, evil, baseness. But cramping the snakes' bodies into tight coils allowed him to imagine potential. He imagined the poison and then imagined it being sucked out of him. He imagined his body rushing blood to the swollen site, the skin pulsing with rejection. He imagined the comforting constriction as the snake pushed out all of his stale air, making him pure and still. In his mind, serpents could compose a braille of salvation on his body. He felt a solidarity with the reptiles. He felt compassion for their status.

John had found a clubbed rattler along the wooded highway one morning and decided to make it his own. He stored it in the freezer for a couple weeks while he finished the squirrel. His fingers stuck to the skin when he pulled the snake out of the freezer, and he let it thaw in the vegetable crisper.

He made his own molds now. When he'd started, he'd ordered them from a taxidermy supply company, but after looking at the shoddy construction, he decided he could very well make them himself by carving thick foam bricks from the hobby shop in town.

He pulled the fangs and the teeth from the mouth of the snake carefully with the Vise-Grip. He knew, from his reading, that the venom that burst from these wounds could remain lethal for years after the snake had died. There were times when he felt light-headed from holding his breath with concentration, and instinct told him to worry it was the snake's toxins acting in revenge, to tread lightly, to be aware.

John selected the manicure scissors from his tray and cut an even split from the vent at the base of the tail, working up to the neck. A snake was either mostly neck, mostly tail, or all abdomen. He couldn't help but fixate on how it didn't matter. He worked his fingers around, peeling the meat from the skin. Occasionally he turned his head away, forcing himself to forget the trembling urges he kept in check.

He trusted in himself and clipped carefully around the mouth, nose, and eyes, a silky slowness to the work. His mind erased the world above the basement, full of bells and smiling ladies, stinging secrets, last rites, sleeping pills. He pushed out names rude with distance, buckling rage, tolerance. He focused only on separating lips from jaw, scraping excess flesh from rind.

He pinned the hide to a board, careful not to stretch it. He waited. He applied oil. He waited. He spun the skin onto its back, applied oil, and waited again. He covered the skin in paper, and placed a board on top, and waited. This went on for days. And while he was waiting, John knit protein powder into blended fruit as he thought about how he didn't want to return to the version of himself who preferred the way the world looked with a scrim of alcohol over it. He checked his shop online and carefully packaged purchased pieces. He wrapped them in the expired free weeklies he retrieved from the library, sealed the boxes precisely with clear tape, labeled them neatly, and walked to the post office, where he greeted Armando by name, and Armando avoided eye contact.

John told himself silently that it wasn't because Armando knew anything of his past, but just because Armando was shy or had too many customers to remember or was interested in maintaining an appearance of strength that didn't allow for small talk. Armando stamped the word FRAGILE onto each box with a willful violence, and John took his receipt and walked home, where he'd look in the mirror as he washed his hands and pause trying to strike a noble pose, like a historical portrait. He googled "shadow people" again but there was only so much to learn. He checked his inbox. He looked for free porn to watch that showed heavy breasts being clutched firmly by fingers with long nails, watching the claws dig into the soft flesh without breaking it, knowing limits, allowing his imagination to bridge the gap, and then he cleared his browser history.

When all of the waiting was through, he brushed the skin lightly, and watched as the scale covers flaked off. This was his dream, to do the same to himself. To lie flat and feel the locked-up shell of him come loose. To pull warmth from the earth when he couldn't make his own. To bundle up his ugliness and allow the world to thieve it from him naturally.

He rinsed the skin delicately in relaxer to keep it moist, and laid it down. He unspooled thick wire the length of the snake and snipped, securing the foam with glue. With a prayer, he slowly fit the skin over the mold of the head, placing tiny balls of clay into the eye sockets, and securing the glass eyes. He packed insulation into the body cavity, sewing it shut as he went along, with confident yet careful pulls of the needle. Just like that, he closed the same body he had opened.

Thinking of this cycle, he decided to make one more change and fit the tail of the finished snake into its own open mouth. He applied glue where the rattle fit into the throat and let his eyes run around and around the circle, singing to himself silently, *I am a problem without a solution. I am a question without an answer. I am a poison without an antidote. I will never know what it is I've done.*

THE PRINCIPAL'S ASHES

ON THE FIRST DAY OF SCHOOL, THE TEACHER
thought only of the first day, not of the 179 to follow.

As the students tip-to-tailed in she looked each of them in the eye. Even if they didn't look back, she could see what she needed to see.

Jonah would be the frogbiter, the child capable of taking away a life. The class frog was sure to die before the end of the year because of Jonah not yet realizing that frogs were alive and capable of feeling pain. Mrs. Sayer had coined the term "frogbiter" in 2005, when little Benny Baft had bitten off a frog's head in an epic tantrum about having to place his fresh set of crayons into the communal box. He'd broken a handful of the wax sticks in half, their soft paper wrappers peeling back as the crayons hit the floor, and then reached into the tank. Mrs. Sayer could have stopped it, but she was tired of cleaning the habitat each week. She watched Benny bite the frog's head off and then crumple with remorse. She picked up the body with a Kleenex, and sent Benny to Principal Fleer, frog blood running down his chin. She'd get hell from the school nurse for not coming along to explain.

Every year this happened, sometimes more brutally than others: bleach in the tank, stapling the frog's hands together, bringing the frog to gym class where he'd be crushed by a basketball. There was always a moment when Mrs. Sayer could have stepped in, but then what? Something else would assail the frog sooner or later. She looked to the event as some sort of harbinger of what the rest of the year held: a groundhog seeing its shadow. The earlier the frog died, the earlier the trouble began.

The last of the children filed in. Sameera returned Mrs. Sayer's gaze and she knew. Sameera would be the one sticking around for a moment after class to ask philosophical questions that Mrs. Sayer didn't have the slightest idea how to answer for a seven-year-old. These were the interactions she took to her Wednesday wine nights with friends: *What do you say when the Muslim child asks you if transubstantiation is real after your religion unit? What do you say when she asks you if you ever worry that the kids are smarter than you? What do you say when she says, "I know you're new at this, but*"? Catholics believe it's real. Every student is smarter than me in some way. I've been doing this for twenty years, actually.

Mrs. Sayer had been raised Catholic. She taught at the Catholic school because it was closer to her house, not because she still believed; half the students in the school weren't even Catholic, and it wasn't as though the ones who were went to church, or believed the Pope was infallible, or cared enough to try to attempt converting the others. Mrs. Sayer sometimes wondered why religion, then, was a part of the required curriculum at all. Why not teach religion at the beginning or end of the day, when the students who were interested could attend? Or send the kids who didn't believe to another elective at that time? Religion, in the context of St. Rosa of the Gardens Elementary, did not provide an education on all of the world's faiths: it was catechism. For the 50 percent of the students who weren't Catholic, it served as a course in lying. They could learn the stories like mythology, and the tenets like ethics, but what about all the bullshit that Catholics believed? That, they had to endure, like getting cornered at a cocktail party by your father-in-law who assumes you agree with everything he's saying. She worried about the children who didn't argue or at least screw up their faces with confusion. Maybe they weren't listening. She soothed herself with this thought.

Ellie T.'s eyes glowed white and centerless. Ellie R. kept her face squeezed shut. Danny Zucco (you couldn't make this up) zapped his eyes around without landing assuredly on any one thing. Elizabeth Harvery appeared to be covered in Vaseline. Sam Stockwell moved in a jerky way, never seeming to touch the floor. Mrs. Sayer had been in this game long enough to remain unconcerned.

After the students had unpacked their backpacks and organized their cubbies, when the children were clear on which hook was theirs in the cloakroom, Mrs. Sayer liked to line the kids up under the auspices of a bathroom break: girls and boys. On the way, they passed an enamel vase outside the school office, just about as tall as the span of Mrs. Sayer's forearm, elbow to wrist. It sat on a little, perfectly sized shelf. A stack of knobs, one on top of the other, capped the vase.

"Who can guess what's in here?" Mrs. Sayer asked.

"Brains?" said Jonah.

"In a way."

"Wishes?" said Sameera.

"You're not wrong," Mrs. Sayer responded.

"A dead cat?" said Kim, whose mother, just that morning, had pulled Mrs. Sayer aside and warned her that Kim's cat had died the week before, and Kim had been morbidly obsessed with it, having dug it up twice already and tried to hide it in her stuffed-animal hammock.

"You might be the closest of all," Mrs. Sayer said, smiling. "Inside this vase are the ashes of our former principal,

Mr. Fleer. Mr. Fleer is watching us all the time, and it is your job, even when my back is turned, to behave in a way that will make Mr. Fleer proud."

The children fidgeted and focused, fidgeted and focused. Mrs. Sayer didn't ask if they had any questions. She knew well that nineteen hands would rocket into the air with unrelated queries. "Let me hear you say, 'Bless us, Mr. Fleer,'" Mrs. Sayer said.

Mr. Allmann passed, wrinkling the wide range between his eyes.

"Wait," Mrs. Sayer said, her eyes on her colleague until he disappeared behind the heavy doors leading to the stairwell. "Okay."

The children shifted their eyes among themselves. "Blefuppmithterflur." It always took a few tries to get the message out clear and concentrated.

As the year progressed, Baldur the frog (only Saint Rosa of the Gardens herself knew where these children learned the things they did) endured, unharmed. Mrs. Sayer answered each of Sameera's questions in such a way that Sameera would smile and nod, temporarily satisfied with her teacher's competence. No scissors cut the palms of hands. No desktops smashed down on fingers. The students abstained from bringing Jell-O cups for their birthday snack after Zaira's presentation on the origins of gelatin, and so there was no need to make fun of Al, the sole vegan. None of the children who knew Santa Claus to be a myth forced their knowledge onto the children who believed. When Mrs. Sayer explained what "waving genitals" were in their poetry unit, no one laughed. It was April, and the class hadn't had to make a repentance visit to Mr. Fleer's ashes.

In the teacher's lounge, Mr. Allmann asked Mrs. Sayer what she was working on that day. Mrs. Sayer sighed.

Every. Single. Goddamned. Day.

"*Howl*," she replied.

"*Howl's Moving Castle* is maybe a little advanced for second-graders, no?" he asked.

"Not *Howl's Moving Castle*," she said. "*Howl*, the Allen Ginsberg poem."

"Oh, I'm not familiar," Mr. Allmann responded, and Mrs. Sayer closed her eyes to hide their rolling.

"They love it," Mrs. Sayer said. "After lunch we're going to perform the poem aloud together. I pass a jug of juice around and everyone takes a sip. The children shout, 'Go go go!' It takes almost an hour."

"Sounds unruly."

"It is," Mrs. Sayer said. "I lock the doors. At least a couple of the sensitive ones will try to escape from the commotion, but that's the lesson. Endurance. Facing the reality of the situation. Finding coping mechanisms."

Mr. Allmann had turned on the faucet to wash his plate,

and Mrs. Sayer could tell he either couldn't hear her or had opted not to.

On her way back to the classroom, Mrs. Sayer nodded to the urn on the wall. Mr. Fleer had been a true model of dedication. He had worked at St. Rosa of the Gardens for the entirety of his career, until the day his heart gave out during a spring choral concert, exploded inside of him at the purity and innocence of the children's voices. His will, prepared well in advance as most things he did were, asked that his ashes might stay in the school itself. Technically the Catholic Church demanded that a person's ashes be buried or entombed as corporeal remains must be, but St. Rosa's was progressive, and for someone who had done as much for the parish as Mr. Fleer had, an exception was made.

Mrs. Sayer had always looked up to Mr. Fleer, but she was also determined not to suffer the same fate he had. Most years it wasn't an issue: the children naturally misbehaved on their own. But this year's class was so composed she saw them as a threat. Her only defense would be to expose them to experience and knowledge beyond their years.

They'd already spent several days breaking down the meaning of each verse line by line. Each child had chosen an image from the poem to draw and Mrs. Sayer had strung the pictures up along the top of the blackboard. (St. Rosa's had

had a fund-raiser to finance whiteboards, but they'd not yet been installed.)

Evie Sharp had drawn money burning in a wastebasket, William Ferris a man jumping off the Empire State Building; Kayla Kamron drew cigarette burns pocking an arm in a surprising shade of blue. Eagle Crowley painted shoes full of blood and Ellen Park took on a visual depiction of "mother finally ******." Simeon Paltz chose to turn in a sound recording of his interpretation of a "catatonic piano." Ellery Chin painted that final image of the door to the cottage on a Western night.

She'd read them the section of *The Dharma Bums* in which Kerouac described the first night Ginsberg read the poem at the Six Gallery. The children bustled, excited for the chance to re-create the event.

Mrs. Sayer was sure the children would get riled. She thought they'd begin to rebel, to tear their books apart, to splash the juice down their shirts, to strike ruler against ruler sparking a fire.

She hoped for nothing less. She wanted to see the children uninhibit themselves. She wanted cause to understand them as imperfect creatures. She wanted to take them down to visit Mr. Fleer's ashes to apologize for the way they'd behaved. She wanted to arrive to the end-of-the-year ceremony knowing she would not drown in the deep well of unpolluted beauty that filled each student.

. . .

Marjana started things off, and the children lolled. They lost interest quickly, and Mrs. Sayer yelled at them to pay attention. She pointed to sections of the room, cueing them to shout and clap and holler in support of the words they heard. She'd spent time coaching each of them individually on pronunciation. They'd notated their sections with indications of where to put the emphasis. Some children followed the key more easily than others. Mrs. Sayer let out a whoop of victory when Cristiana Gutierrez finally pronounced "yacketayakking" correctly. She mouthed along "bop kabbalah" with Joe Swearingen, and felt it was to her credit that he finally teased it out without pausing.

She'd assigned the line about "the one eyed shrew that does nothing but sit on her ass and snip the intellectual golden threads of the craftsman's loom" to Edward Sharma. She could tell he was already well aware of everything in the world that threatened to leave him with nothing.

She knew it would cause waves that she gave the entire Moloch section to Seraphine Bailey, but good god that girl could read at a fifth-grade level, and adrenaline scrambled through Mrs. Sayer. The girl ratcheted up her volume as the second section proceeded, until, unbidden, Seraphine unlatched the window and shouted "into the street!" right onto the playground where the afternoon kindergarteners looked up in wonder.

Mrs. Sayer saw it as a sign from heaven that the last section of the poem had nineteen repetitions of "I'm with you in Rockland," the number of kids in the class, and each of the children, alert, hovering over their chairs, voiced their part without prompting. The juice sat unfinished, the classroom undestroyed. Mrs. Sayer was proud of their composure, but also disappointed. She *wanted* to visit Mr. Fleer, and so, when the poem wrapped in on itself, she let the silence hold for a moment, deciding what to do.

Outside the principal's office, beneath the urn, Mrs. Sayer told the class, "Mr. Fleer thought you were capable of more, children." She pinged between their faces, still flushed with the exertion of the performance. "Mr. Fleer was counting on you to rebel. Mr. Fleer wanted to see your true nature accelerate out of your soft, stretching bodies, but you failed him today."

✦

AT THE ASSEMBLY on the last day of classes, when parents file up to thank Mrs. Sayer for her service, not one of them will inquire as to why she thought it would be appropriate to teach their children a poem about the way the ethical emergencies of the 1950s caused people's minds to falter. Even Rara's mother won't complain about how her daughter walks around the house repeating a couplet that contains the word "ass." Instead, they will shake her hand and pass her Starbucks gift cards in folded cardboard, bearing the names of their children in a hand too steady to be authentic. When a parent complains about how hot it is in the gym, Mrs. Sayer will stop herself from telling them the world will become uninhabitable before their children's natural lives end. Instead, she will say, "And it's only June," as though the weather were as inexplicable as the Holy Trinity.

Mrs. Sayer will take the last gift card from Jonah, the child she'd identified as the frogbiter, though Baldur still hops around his tank. She will stare into his eyes and wonder how she ever could have thought he was a murderer.

"My favorite Starbucks is chocolate milk," Jonah will say.

When Mrs. Sayer's heart stops, she'll realize she'd been right all along.

DON'T LET'S

WHEN I WENT OUT INTO THE KITCHEN TO AS-
sess the damage from the night before, I saw the neat line
I'd made of PBR cans along the counter and a half-eaten bag
of generic sandwich cookies. Even in my stupor, I tended
toward the tidy. The front porch faced the marshland. An
old rattan couch and a slatted wood bench served as the
only living-room-like area for the ranch house. The Georgia
low country counted on year-round decent weather for its
relaxing.

On the bench sat the empty tuna can I'd used as an
ashtray the night before. I smoked only when drunk. To

discourage myself, I rolled the worst tobacco I could find, as thinly as possible.

Beside the can I found a fat, messy cigarette barely holding itself together, and looked around like I might see the person who had made it. I took it apart and shook the tobacco back into the pouch.

I'd wanted some time to clear my head. All my friends told me to go to a beach or some city in Europe where I didn't know the language, so I could tune out and sightsee and avoid letting myself think too much, but with the cast on my leg, water wasn't really an option and I didn't have the budget for a transatlantic flight.

I booked the ranch house out in the swampland because it was a landscape I hadn't spent time in before, but it was warm—a nice break from winter up north. The house was tiny and the rent cheap, but the land it stood on stretched for acres. Live oaks reached their tentacles from their low wide bases up toward the sky and the gray Spanish moss, like gentle barbed wire, never swayed in the slightest, the air was so still. Resurrection ferns covered every inch of tree bark so that the landscape looked vibrant and green now, but on the day I'd arrived the region had still been waiting out a period of drought, and the leaves appeared shriveled and dead. I was shocked at how the area came to life the next day when the rains fell. Green buds showed up next to brown leaves on the oaks. I was used to pausing for a whole winter while the trees revitalized, but the South, it seemed, operated on an accelerated cycle of growth and decay. Palmettos filled in the underbrush and every time I grazed one, the percussive reverberation through its fans convinced me some wild beast was tracking close behind.

To get to the property, you had to enter a code at a low wooden gate, more deterrent than barrier.

The house's porch and shutters were painted a color I'd learned was called "haint blue," a shade meant to keep the ghosts away. The email I'd received from the owners said the key was hidden under the turtle shell on the windowsill. "We don't lock our doors when we're there. We've never experienced crime, but we also can't be held responsible for theft of any of your belongings, so lock the house if you're leaving expensive items for a long period of time."

I hadn't seen anyone on the inside of the gate since I'd loaded in, but I saw a couple other rentals on the property. They'd told me neither had been leased for the time I was supposed to be here; I had the place all to myself.

I washed out the empties and dropped them in the recycling bin. The vaulted kitchen made the place feel open. Behind the spinning ceiling fan, a small door led to what I assumed was an attic space stretching over the rest of the house.

After I hobbled back from the recycling bin, I leaned against the counter and saw that that little door was now open. I tried to be reasonable. A breeze could be to blame. Humidity might have unstuck it. Still, I thought about seeking out a ladder, before remembering it'd be sure death to try to climb with only my right foot. I raised on a single tiptoe, bracing myself on the crutches, but only a thin line of darkness wedged itself into the exposed space. And what did I think I'd find anyway? Something that had let itself in or out? With two empty rentals on the property, who would go to the trouble of messing with the attic of the only house that was inhabited?

I told myself I was paranoid, that I was letting the events of the past few weeks get to me. I told myself it would be best if I got out of the house for a while.

I drove into town and bought some chicken necks. The owners had left a binder full of all sorts of ideas on how to make the most of the area. "If you put chicken necks in the crab trap down by the dock, you can get yourself a mighty fine dinner for cheap."

I didn't see what all the fuss was about crab, honestly, but I didn't have much else to do.

I didn't know how to prepare crabs and should have looked it up before I got to the store, but I picked up some garlic and a bag of potatoes. All the onions felt a little too soft, but I grabbed one of those anyway and lined up everything on the conveyor belt.

"Bring me a few of those crabs," the cashier said, scanning the chicken necks.

"We'll see how I do," I told her.

I'd brought my own shopping bag and she set the items

in it carefully. "Don't lose this," she said, handing me the pharmacy receipt crumpled in the bottom of the tote. The coupons attached to the receipt had already expired, but I thanked her and headed home.

I swung myself across the property to the dock, book tucked under my chin. At the bank, I debated the best way to get down to the water. The ramp was about the height and steepness of a flight of stairs, and rather than pitching myself headfirst down the incline, I sat on my butt and scooted down, the package of chicken necks in one hand. I ripped open the plastic and pinched each piece of meat, dropping them into the trap. I wondered if I'd die of some sort of bacterial infection if I didn't traipse back up to the house to wash my hands. I kicked the trap into the marsh and leaned my torso over the edge of the dock to splash my fingers in the water.

After inching backward up the ramp, I gathered the crutches and the book I'd left on the landing above. I struggled to stand and made my way to the hammock strung between two sandy pines. When I turned the page, I saw a man standing thirty feet away at the corner of my vision, but I focused left and saw it was just a boat tarp slung over a pole.

I read, squinting against the bright sun, trying to stay alert, but eventually gave in to the drift and dozed until I heard a loud tearing sound and peered around the bend in the water. About a block away a piece of the old tabby cane mill ruins was breaking off and sliding into the river below. I'd read about this in one of the articles in the house binder. The ruins, made of oyster shells, ash, and sand, had stood for over two hundred years, had been pummeled of their purpose by hurricane winds in the 1800s, and had been breaking down slowly ever since. You could buy property on which the ruins stood, but because they were on the historic register, you couldn't technically own the ruins themselves. If a person wanted to wander onto your property to see them, that was legal, but there was no effort being made to save them, so as trees died and the soil loosened, the banks receded and the ruins crumpled into the marsh. Even then it wasn't legal to move the ruins from the water, but boat motors caught on the ruins' stones as they passed, and rumor was, late at night, the locals set out on expeditions to haul up the most unwieldy pieces to move them aside or drop them off at a friend's place for covert safekeeping.

I stood and watched as a wide piece of the wall tumbled forward into the middle of the waterway, its thin end sticking out of the marsh. High tide would hide it beneath the surface and I cringed at the thought of one of the small motorboats that shuttled through tearing its hull on the chunk, unaware of the need to steer around a new threat.

I made my way down to the dock and pulled on the rope I'd tied to the pier. It took a moment for me to find my leverage, sitting on the ground like that, but when I hauled the trap up, three brown crabs grapevined inside. I wasn't sure I could eat one crab, let alone three. I opened the elaborate series of doors and froze, trying to figure out if there was an art to freeing them. I reached my hand in, but the crabs waved their claws like they knew what they were in for. I turned the trap over and tried to shake them out. Two of the creatures scrambled out easily, the smell of them overwhelmingly foul, and I pinched them into a bucket stationed on the dock for this reason. The last clung to the inside of the cage. I thought about just leaving it on the dock with the door open and hoping it might get free on its own, but I took a chance and pushed on the claw stuck to the outer edge of the metal, and the last crab rattled free. I dropped him back into the water, and then I looked into the bucket at the others and pitched them over the side of the dock, too.

On Tuesday, I heard something rifling around outside my bedroom and my mind raced. I didn't know whether to keep still or try to scare the something away. I looked around my room for a weapon, but came up short. I grabbed the lamp off the end table and tried to maneuver the plug from the outlet behind the bed. By then the sound had quieted, but I cracked the door anyway. Something big and dark bounded down the hall, stopping just short and nudging the door open wider. I put down the lamp and held out my fingers to the Great Dane. He rubbed his snout into my hand and I slapped his flank.

"Mason? Hello? Is Mason in here?"

I made my way to the front door, Mason beside me, and saw a man in work clothes.

"Aw, there he is," he said, clucking his tongue to call the dog to him. "Mason, I bet you scared this lady half to death." He turned to me. "I'm so sorry. We used to live here and at some point he figured out how to open this front door. I look after the property when the Mitchells aren't here. John." He held out his hand.

I shook it and smiled. "How did he learn to open doors?" We both looked at the knob.

"Damned if I know," he said. "He knows better than to do it when I'm watching. He ran on ahead while I was looking at a faucet in the house across the way. My apologies, again."

"Not at all," I said. "He was just a bit of a surprise."

"I'm sure he was," he said. "Come on, Mason. Time for us to head out! Leave this lady in peace." He turned to give a wave.

"There's no one in the other houses now, right?" I asked. I hadn't even known I wanted to ask it until it was out of my mouth.

"Nope, you're alone here, except when me and Mason show up to give you a scare."

"Thanks," I said.

"Take care, now." He shut the door behind him.

That night, I made mac and cheese out of the box and ate it in bed watching *Dateline*, until I realized the episode was about a woman who was convinced someone else was living in her house with her, sleeping when she was awake, leaving sloppy clues behind. I turned it off, and when I couldn't fall right asleep I cursed myself for finishing off the dregs of that pot of coffee in the afternoon. I tossed around and thought I heard something in the attic above me, a gentle scuttling, like a rat. I told myself it was probably a piece of the Spanish moss dusting the roof and let my mind loosen and relax. I startled awake when I heard what I thought might be the front door opening and waited, but I didn't hear anything else. I stared at the curtain and tried to find the crack of light along the edges, but the darkness was so total, I couldn't tell when my eyes were open or closed.

I woke gasping a deep drink of humidity like it was no air at all and looked around. The curtain hung to one side, light elbowing in.

I felt an ache rummage through my bones and I reached for the crutches and struggled to stand. I balanced on one leg and pulled my arms above my head and to the sides, trying to work out the fatigue. I saw a small gap in the window frame I hadn't noticed before. I put my hand to it, but couldn't even fit a fingertip through the space between where the frame met the molding. I reached over to my bedside table and grabbed a cotton ball and wedged it into the crack. Better safe than sorry I'd swallowed a dozen spiders, I thought.

The binder told me I should try the seafood at a restaurant a half hour away. I looked everywhere for the key to the house, but couldn't find it in my bag or on the table near the door. I left the house unlocked, reminding myself the owners did it all the time.

The restaurant's website said to be sure to follow their directions, and I was thankful for this reassurance when I was instructed to turn down what seemed like a person's driveway.

I opened the screen door and it slammed quickly behind me. A woman in plain clothes, with a Band-Aid on her nose, winced at the smack-rebound-smack of the door. "Good morning," she said. I noticed a pink car seat balanced on the table in front of her.

"I'm so sorry!" I whisper-shouted. "Did I wake her?"

"No, no," she said, waving her hand, speaking full-voice. "She's a weird kid. My first grandbaby. Have to get just the right kind of music on the radio and then she just falls asleep. Today it's mariachi, I guess. Sorry about that. Sit anywhere you like."

I took a seat at a plastic-covered table near the front and glanced around for the bar I'd seen in the photos online.

"Can I get you something to drink, hon? Pepsi product? Sweet tea? I've got a full bar."

I felt relief when she said "full bar." I'd planned on ordering a whiskey or a beer, but I chickened out. Her greeting of "Good morning" had made me self-conscious. "A sweet tea," I said, like it had been my plan all along. She dropped a menu in front of me, hot-pink legal-sized paper with eight items written in Sharpie, each separated by a thick black line. I closed my eyes and landed a finger on the paper to choose.

I'd been mulling over whether to come here for lunch or dinner and, looking around, I regretted my decision. The place was empty and I'd been hoping to make a few temporary friends.

She returned with my sweet tea and asked if I was ready to order.

"The fried shrimp, please," I said.

"Fries and coleslaw okay?" she asked.

I lingered on the option of hush puppies, but nodded.

She went back to the kitchen. I heard a refrigerator open. I heard the slide of a metal tub on a steel countertop. I heard her bracelets jangle as she shook whatever it was free of its container.

When she came back out, she was on the phone. "I really let Rhonda have it the other night . . . You know they finally got rid of the big wine glasses because we were so low on them and she's been filling the small ones clear up to the rim, so I'm dripping wine on everyone . . . Yeah, I know. I think she understands now . . . I won't have to tell her twice, no . . . Okay, hon. I'll see y'all soon."

She stood at the door, looking out. "At least there's a little bit of a breeze today."

I felt no such thing. The movement of the leaves on the trees was barely perceptible, but I agreed, willing to accept that this was what passed for wind in the low country.

She went back to the kitchen to retrieve my shrimp and presented the platter to me. I noticed a hush puppy hiding under the pile of french fries. I looked up at her in thanks, and she said, "It's lucky. Make a wish." She stood at the door again and noticed my license plate out front. "Just passing through?" she asked.

"I'm staying a couple weeks over on the cane mill property in Meridian."

"Oh, how's that? You like it there?"

"I do," I said. "It's very secluded. Real quiet and peaceful." I registered the small shifts in my inflection, inching closer to her accent.

"They say there's ghosts there, you know. Slave ghosts. All those irrigation ditches dug by Gullah. They call it a cane mill property, but you realize that was a plantation, right?"

I had. I'd wondered if it was wrong of me to stay there. I worried I was paying money to plantation heirs, but the property had foreclosed a decade before. "Yes," I said solemnly, hoping I was indicating the respect I had for the history of the place.

"You seen any of those ghosts?" she asked.

I shook my head.

"No boo hag come for you in the night?" she asked with a laugh.

I shook my head again.

"You don't know the boo hag?" she asked. "That's Gullah. Like a bogeyman or, or a—a—a vampire, but they don't take your blood. They take your breath."

I hoped she'd go on.

"They come in through a crack or a hole in the wall. They're red because they don't have skin, see? And they come in the night and hover over you and steal your breath. If you struggle, they'll take your skin and put it on."

The woman noticed me thinking. "What? It's just a story. You scare easy."

"I've gotten myself nervous out there all alone. I think I hear things in the house and this morning I woke up and I couldn't catch my breath," I said. "You're saying the right things."

The woman came closer and chucked my arm. "Ooh, you got a boo hag! You know what the old lore used to say you should do? You get a broom and put it by your bed. Then the boo hag will be distracted and try to count all the straw instead of stealing your energy."

I laughed at this. "The evil boo hag just doesn't stand a chance if there's a broom to get to counting with!" I said, and the woman laughed, too.

"It's the air, hon. The humidity down here catches up with you. You just enjoy yourself and forget all those stories." She went back to check on the baby in the carrier and I looked out at the ripples on the water. A truck pulled up outside to make a delivery and the driver greeted me and apologized for the open door, but I didn't see any harm in it.

When I paid up, I thanked the woman.

"Don't let the boo hag ride ya," she said, as I stepped

out. "That's what the Gullah say. 'Don't let the boo hag ride ya.'"

I waved and shut the door quietly behind me.

Cliff had never hit me. He'd never choked me. He'd never grabbed me and he didn't own a gun. One time when he was drunk, I woke up to him trying to push my head into his lap in the middle of the night. It was only scary because his dick was hard, which made the situation feel more real. He was uncoordinated in his sleep, though. I shoved him hard and took all the blankets out to the couch to sleep, leaving him naked on the fitted sheet in the dead of winter.

When he woke up I told him what he'd done and he cried. He couldn't believe the violence that lived in him, but I could. He promised never to drink again and I felt annoyed by this. I liked to drink. I didn't want to feel like we couldn't go to bars or that we had to leave parties by 11:00 p.m. when he started to get sleepy without liquor to keep him riled. He was socially quiet enough as it was; at least a drink or two loosened him up. But his fear of hurting me held him true to his word.

When I tried to open the door to my bedroom in the ranch house, it wouldn't budge. I panicked for a moment. If I were locked out of my room, who would let me back in? And if I were locked out, and a boo hag was pursuing me down the hall, how would I defend myself? By not breathing? I told myself I was joking, but the joke cut my fear, and I needed it.

I jiggled the handle on the door and remembered the lock had been installed upside down and all I needed to do was turn it the opposite way.

I leaned my crutches against the wall and flopped onto the bed and lay there for a whole minute before fear forced me up again. I ambled to the kitchen to retrieve a broom and prop it beside the bed. It felt like tempting fate not to comply with a solution so easy.

I poured myself a bourbon and sank it into my shirt pocket, and limped out to the gazebo on the water. I rocked one-footed in my chair and watched the marsh grass wave with a breeze I couldn't feel. The chairs alongside me tipped forward and back like I wasn't alone at all. Only being able to transport one drink at a time was probably for the best. If I had much more than that I was sure to bite it on my way back through the pinecone-strewn yard with its sandy divots and fungus-thick sinkholes. The night snuck up quickly and I managed to waddle back, tucking my cell phone as a flashlight in the pocket of my shorts.

I dredged the fish fillet I'd bought at the market in flour and battled with the electric range, downing one more whiskey while I ate. That night either the broom worked to deter the boo hag or the drink had carried me deep enough into sleep that I didn't notice my breath being pulled from me.

In the morning I woke up feeling oxygenated, if a bit hungover. I still had my bra on under my T-shirt and my hand was tingly from the way I'd curled my wrist below my pillow. But when I finally hauled myself from bed and shuffled one-footed to the kitchen to put the coffee on, I saw movement out in the small pond in the front yard. I leaned closer to the glass, trying to see what was in the water. In an agitated thrash, an alligator, maybe four feet, leapt at a bird near the edge of the pond. Even with the wall separating us, I felt adrenaline rush through. If there was one alligator, there could be many more around here, and I was not at my fastest right now.

I picked up my phone, and realized I had no idea who to call for help. I tried the owners of the property first, but they didn't pick up. I wished I had the number of the groundskeeper who'd stopped by with his dog, but I did not. Was I supposed to call Animal Control or a private service? I found a removal company and called the number, but they said I was out of their zone. They gave me the number of a second company, who said they could be out in the next two hours.

I sat on a stool, waiting for the alligator to move again, but it didn't. I began to tell myself I might have imagined it. When two men in khaki work clothes walked up, they stood tall trying to see into the pond from a distance. They said something to each other and moved toward the door. I stumbled off the stool to let them in. "Thank you so much for coming," I said.

The taller guy waved his hand like it was nothing. "He's not so big. We'll trap him and take him away."

"What happens after that?" I asked, afraid of the answer.

"Don't worry. If we were gonna kill him, we wouldn't go to the trouble of trapping him. We'll set him free down the river and hope he doesn't find his way back."

I hoped the same and thanked them for coming so quickly. "Do you need me out there with you for any reason?"

The shorter guy eyed my crutches. "In your state you'd only be useful as bait. We've got this."

I took my place at the stool again and watched as the shorter guy monitored the alligator while the taller guy readied the trap. I wondered if I should offer them the left-over chicken necks I had in the fridge, but they packed what looked like some sort of hearts into the far end of the cage.

The shorter guy took a long stick from the truck and the taller guy stood back. The shorter guy positioned himself behind the trap, and reached the stick around to nudge the alligator. The alligator whipped its head around, but didn't move. It flexed its jaw open. I couldn't hear much behind the glass, but I imagined a hiss or a growl. The men laughed and I wondered if the laughter was nerves or amusement or both.

The shorter man poked the gator again, and this time it clambered out of the water. It looked so goofy the way it moved, like it had no idea how to do what it was doing. The alligator paused and caught sight of the meat in the trap and waited. When it pounced, the shorter man jumped back, unsure if the reptile might be aiming for the trap or for him. The door snapped shut on the cage and the men, in unison, turned to me to give a thumbs-up. I wondered how many alligators you had to trap before you could turn your back on them so confidently. I registered the men grinning at me proudly, but my eyes stayed trained on the gator. The men used some sort of tweezer-shaped tool to push a rubber band through the grates of the cage to wrap around the animal's mouth. I knew from reading placards at zoos that alligators have an enormous amount of strength in the muscles used to close their jaws, but the muscles they used to open them were pitifully weak. A regular old rubber band could keep an alligator's mouth shut. Once they'd muzzled the animal, the taller man reached in to tie a blindfold around the beast's eyes and the shorter man returned to the front door.

"What's with the blindfold? Is that how you make sure he doesn't find his way back?" I was half joking, but the man had clearly heard this one before.

He didn't crack a smile and his response had no music in it. "It calms them, so they don't lash out as much. That'll be three hundred dollars. We accept all major credit cards, cash, or check," he said, without missing a beat.

I realized I'd at least have to front the money, but wondered if the owners might decline to reimburse me. After all, it wasn't their fault an alligator crawled into their pond.

In any case, I couldn't have stayed if the alligator remained and I couldn't have left, either. I felt like I'd done a lot of surviving these past few weeks, but I hobbled to my purse and pulled out my Mastercard, throwing money I didn't have at the problem. The guy typed the numbers into his phone and had me sign with my finger.

I saw him out and stood in the doorway until the truck was out of sight, then looked back at the pond, searching for evidence of lingering danger.

When I drove around the area, I did double takes, whipping my eyes between the wealthy homes and the run-down clapboard houses whose lawns were strewn with plastic tubs and mechanical parts and soaked stuffed animals, half dressed in layers of moss.

At a shrimp shop I asked the waitress if this town was on its way up or down.

"Up, I think," she said. "What do you mean?"

I told her about all the new construction I saw alternated with rows of trailers in bad need of repair.

"Oh, that happens because of *the help*. You catch my drift?"

I tried to make it work in my head. "I understand they'd have to live somewhere, but wouldn't they live in a different neighborhood? Everything's so evenly mixed."

"No, no. You see, the help would live right behind the houses where they worked, but then when that ended, all of those houses stayed mixed up."

I nodded. I thought of those ditches on the property, of the way fog settled into them in the morning when the sun was coming up, hiding the way the ground disappeared into nothing.

Everyone kept saying that he only did it because he was drunk. "He hasn't acted like that since he got sober," they said. "He was set off."

I had a different theory. I thought people acted *more* like themselves when they were drunk. Of all the times I'd had one or ten too many, I looked back at what I could remember of the night and recognized the impulses in each of the actions I'd taken. When I asked my best friend if she really wanted her baby when it was due only a week later, that was a question that had lingered in my mind already, one I'd almost voiced just a day, a week, a month before. A drink just tipped me into asking it out loud. When I kissed that man at the bar who said he was married, I'd already talked to Cliff about what it might mean for us to open our relationship. "Just for an occasional fling," I'd said. "Just to play that game sometimes." He'd said it would be fine with him as long as we were honest with each other. I'd realized that wasn't a green light but I knew my actions would be defensible.

With my hand on the thigh of that married man, I saw Cliff order a double Maker's. I saw him down it in a gulp. A part of me was happy he was drinking again. I got tired of flirting with the man after he slipped his wedding ring in his pocket, as if he thought it was standing in my way, as if he thought it served as anything but an incentive. When he asked if I wanted to go somewhere, I told him I did: to my own home, alone. I told Cliff I was leaving; we'd driven separately. "Stay. Have fun," I said.

Cliff didn't want to ask if the guy was coming with me. He flipped bills onto the bar for one more and grabbed his jacket.

I rolled over and felt a warmth beside me, like a body had just vacated the spot or the sun had been shining. The room was dark. I let myself wonder.

The door beside the ceiling fan was wide open when I poured myself cereal. I went to the yard and whispered my call to the police, asking if they'd mind sending someone just to check it out. "I'm sure it's nothing, but I'm incapacitated at the moment, and I'd appreciate the peace of mind," I said.

The operator laughed. "It's no trouble," she said. "We're a quiet county. Okay if I send Bill over after lunch?" I was thankful that she understood my lack of urgency, and made my way to the barn to be sure I could point at a ladder the officer could use to get up to the space.

The officer arrived around 11:00 and I wondered how early he ate lunch or if he'd decided he preferred to get his work done beforehand.

He hauled the ladder in and demonstrated an assured nonchalance as he climbed the rungs, like he knew there would be nothing up there.

"Just some old boxes," he said.

I tried to stop myself, but asked, "No blankets that look like a makeshift bed or anything?"

"Nope, it's pretty empty up there," he said. He collapsed the ladder and carried it back out to the barn. "I know how women can freak themselves out staying alone in the middle of nowhere," he said. "Try to enjoy the quiet."

I resented that I'd served as a reinforcement of his stereotype. I wanted to erase my request for help. I wanted to tell him what I thought of his theories.

When Cliff had pulled out of the parking lot behind me, when he'd bumped his truck up against my hatchback trying to get me to pull over, I saw what he'd done as an indication of what he cared to do with my body if he could get me out of the hard shell of the vehicle.

For a minute I was relieved that he was letting his jealousy show through. I felt like finally we might get somewhere, until I slowed for a turn and he gunned his engine right into my driver's-side door.

The binder told me there was a community of the last Gullah people out on one of the barrier islands, but even the idea of visiting exhausted me.

I poured a drink and slid it into my pocket and swung out to the porch. I settled the glass on the table and reached over to look under the turtle shell. The key was there, but it wasn't my doing. I grabbed it and slid it into the pocket of my shorts, and plopped down onto the couch.

I didn't press charges against Cliff, but his lawyers told him vehicular assault was a possibility if I had. All that and Cliff never apologized.

When I moved my stuff out, I felt angry that I was the one having to find a new home, but I knew it would be easier that way.

A friend packed my last carload while I wobbled around the house, not yet used to the crutches, still trying to put my foot down out of habit.

"You're wasting your time moving your stuff out," Cliff said. "You're just going to have to bring it all back when you come to your senses."

I didn't see that fit to respond to, and left the door open behind me so he'd need to get up and close it after I'd gone.

When I looked out at the marsh, the water seemed higher than I'd remembered. For a moment I wondered if I'd exaggerated the distance from the bank down to the dock, but then I remembered that the tides brought the water in twice a day. The moon pulled the swamp around, forcing me to see it differently.

I thought of how Cliff had apologized all those years ago when I'd told him how he'd treated me in his sleep, but how he couldn't feel sorry this time around, when he knew exactly what he'd done.

I thought of the boo hag now, how it crept in, how it took your energy if you were still, but stole your skin if you struggled. I didn't move a muscle.

GET BACK

VILLARD TOOK MY GRACE WITH AN UNDONE, half-paralyzed anger, and so I found him daily and burned his house down on what I deemed a repeated whim. Jean told the world I was nutty, scouring my freedom for black marks, and so I broke his teeth back and forth on many rainbows of oily asphalt. Claus opened my door, not knowing it was my door, and so I hand-plucked each hair from his scalp for what seemed like days. Paul swore spite upon my family; I knocked him on the head so hard his thoughts never again amounted to more than clouds. Herman smiled at the wrong time, and so I futzed up his nethers with weird knives, moving his muscles around carelessly. Jacques intervened briefly, and I gave him a nasty version of a baptism with ugly fluids wept from the sores of the other prisoners. Simon showed early willfulness by calling me stupid, and so I punched him hard in his calm heart. Jean returned with his crumpled mouth, to make more out of what was nothing, and I burst my fist into his eye socket with a dazzle. Nicolas wonked about when he was on duty; I took his simple feelings and drove them down his throat.

Up inside of me, the dread kept smoking. How long would I feel this urge to seek justice on those who did me even minor wrongs? I kept whispering to myself that I'd relax after all was righted, but I kept exacting these filthy retributions.

Antoine hammered me for forgiveness, but still I dragged him through his own goodwill, kicking and screaming. Jean, again, having allowed me to destroy him twice already, spoke of his children, vowed for them with purpose, but I took their happy little family of self-righteous brilliance and promised to scale them one by one. When Jean heard this intention, he hid, leaving his daughters in my hands. This cowardice caused the sick to rise in me, and I held the first girl closer, snorting, sanctioning Jean to observe the intimacy of my destruction from his warren, allowing him to imagine I'd stop at blinding her, and then erasing his reverie. Nicolas returned, repentant for his scatter. I killed him like it was a novelty, like I was paying empty tribute, and hung his face on my wall. Franklin shouldered a secret to me, thinking he could gain my trust with nonsense; I turned his tomorrows to yesterdays. Ligier dripped his mongering thoughts on me, and I pepped up, acknowledging his delirium by digging up his organs with spectacular slowness.

The desire arises from the satisfaction. Like an addict knowing exactly what awaits him, I look for more ways to re-create the feeling of the first time. I cuddle the fear and death close to me like a comfort. I say, "Must I?" and affirm myself.

Philibert was so-so, and this seemed enough reason to pike his loins. Pierre was the victim of two different swindlers, and this weakness disgusted me. He shared his affections, and I showed him how base I found him by taking possession of all of his fingers and stringing them on a length of hemp. I thought of Jean and his dirt-ceilinged fate. I thought of his daughters arranged around him like sunbeams in the burial plot. I thought of the taste of their tears as I licked them from the blade of my knife. Truth seeped through. I thought of the room waiting for Jacques at the asylum, small and the same every day for the rest of his life. I elegantly detached Pierre's fingernails from the string of dead flesh and tiled a tiny box, which I presented to him the next day. I broke through the judgment made on Antoine and used my own. I leaned in to him and said, "It is I, your forward intimate. You of the drooling class have elected yourself to the privacy of an execution. I, of the more syllabled humanity, am pointing my finger. It is your time." He went oil-tongued, as his body slid beneath the bridge of the table.

It was a turnstile of dead bodies. One would think my conscience would shriek at the steadfast profusion, the illegal disease of communion I granted each man. I was captured by the empty smoke of the crematory. I could no longer smell the damage of the loose women or the misdirection of the determined perverts. I gawked and groped for some of the impulses that led to the coals. I gulped the spinning exorcisms in the air. I waxed on the impropriety until I made fictions. The severity of this swinging spectrum of justice kicked my balance out from under me, my nerves intact, yet newly sabotaged. A channel, a galley, a passage through the chicken-wire throughways of me, the increasing margins of my message, the mirrored whirling of coarse disaster, the dissolution of sin and the hope for happiness at last.

Jehan was bold and armed. An icon of exotic life and fearful decadence. He used his girth and draping nets of sentimentality as his unparalleled excuse, and I gave out explicit commands: the trilling snap of his spine and unthrottled gush as all his body held let loose upon his parlor floor. Germain fled, and when I caught him I formed cataracts on his earthly joy.

. . .

Some believe good must triumph over evil. Some think we must void ourselves of both, to achieve a perfect emptiness. Some insist that evil is just the lack of good, that evil doesn't even exist.

I believe in the permanence of the tide. I conceive of an inundating gravity. I find within myself a belief that the trawling winds of mortality should be turned upon the unworthy. I call myself a fluctuating compass of destiny. There is power in the fall of these verdicts. There is a price to such dismissals. The fields sigh with their chorus of pity, as the open land becomes dappled with the freshly turned soil of graves. It is only a constant chronology that has brought us here. Death is but a scar. I empty the clocks. I swallow the skeleton keys.

PASTORAL

Featuring Lines from Virgil's *Eclogues*
and Theocritus's "Idyll 1"

THE SMELL OF THE POWDER RELEASED IN A PUFF on our faces, my third-favorite scent, commenced the alchemy. While getting our makeup done, Dave and I usually talked about our kids. He was such a kind man, and his priorities were clear. His family came first and fucking came second.

Feed, swains, your oxen as of old; rear your bulls.

I would tell Dave about my sons: one delicate and one a bruiser, but both boisterous in the right mood. He'd tell me about how his daughter liked to scream, "Be murdered, Daddy!" and somehow that would translate to him shrieking for minutes on end. "Should I be concerned?" Dave asked me, and we both cackled. Kids would be kids.

. . . heartsick, I myself am driving my goats along . . .

Once we were made up and ready to go, we'd get a few minutes alone together. The director and crew left the set, and Dave and I sat on the couch together. He ran his hand down my cheek, and I leaned in and we kissed. We could mean it and still be in love with our partners back home. It felt healthy and professional, like we were good at our jobs.

For these have we sown our fields!

Dave pulled apart my robe and pushed my tits together and sighed and I saw his robe part to make way for evidence of his admiration. It was always at this point that the director would call out to ask if it was safe for him to return. "They must have cameras on us, right?" Dave said, with a big boyish smile. I shrugged. It didn't make what we had any less real.

. . . wooing the woodland Muse on slender reed . . .

"What's on the docket for today, Coach?" I asked.

. . . fling these artless strains to the hills and woods . . .

The director looked at his shot list. "As you can see, this one's set outdoors. We've got a few trees and some boulders set up with grass. We'll shoot externals out at a creek tomorrow. Kim, you're Alexis, the object of Corydon's—that's you, Dave—the object of Corydon's desire. You should be attentive but withholding. Alexis—I'll call you by your characters' names—you're actually just a figment of Corydon's imagination, but that won't be clear until the end. We'll take care of that in After Effects. Corydon, you'll watch Alexis frolic some, to start. Alexis, you're enjoying the nature that surrounds you. We'll green-screen in a background soon, but feel free to see your body as an extension of the landscape, to be enjoyed. Corydon, after watching from this corner over here for a while, stroking yourself, approach Alexis. Alexis, you'll never acknowledge Corydon fully. No eye contact. Enjoy the way Corydon touches you, manipulates you, as though it were all a part of your fantasy. We're thinking some harmless making out. Then some rear penetration leaning on a boulder. After that, Corydon, you're going to ask Alexis if she's been bad. Alexis, still no answer. Corydon, you take that as a yes and apply some discipline: nothing too much, just some slaps, spanking maybe, Dave— sorry, Corydon—you hold her arms down. Once you're through with that, some postcoital cuddling. Corydon, you'll ask Alexis her name; Alexis, still no answer. Go back to the make-out. Alexis, we'll erase you from his arms in post, and Corydon, you'll realize, gradually, that you're alone, but Alexis's toga will be on the ground. Rub your cock as a remembrance, tenderly, and that will be that. Manny, bring in the sheep!" the director called behind him. He turned to us. "No animal play. Let's keep this clean."

Sooner, then, shall the nimble stag graze in air, and the seas leave their fish bare on the strand.

I shivered with excitement. What luck was this? To have a decent plot, a director who didn't force a script on us and trusted us to make the moves look natural, a beautiful co-star with bare appeal. An assistant brought out my costume, a humble elegy to a toga. One tit mumbled behind fabric while the other glowed heavy in the lights. I looked across the stage at Dave, also being authenticated with a short frock. His nodding dick lifted the hem. Our gazes embraced across the room, a lush charm filling the space between.

The mirror never lies.

When we stepped on set, and the lights shined us bright, I felt like the elusive nymph I was supposed to play. I felt a true course of yearning experienced. "Alexis!" the director called out. "You look like a Greek statue! If a Greek statue were made of the most sumptuous human flesh you could imagine." I kept in character. Approached Dave with his cocked package. Availed him of my bared breast. Hung a small smile between us, then depressed it. Tore at his confidence with my teeth. Hosted the control in this situation.

Pushed the jealousy into him. Then gave him a doll-like welcome. I dropped to my knees. Belted nature with my mouth. Conjured from him a rigid stammer. Tingling. Panting. Simplifying.

Ah, lovely boy, trust not too much to your bloom!

When we finish filming, I shower because I know I should, but I linger a bit in front of my mirror, wiping off my makeup and examining my pores, reveling in the smell of Dave and lube and the sweat of the work we've done. Ahead of that first puff of powder before a shoot, this is my first-favorite smell.

. . . the copses under the burning sun echo my voice with that of the shrill cicadas.

There are no wolves at the door. No natural disaster waits in the clouds or beneath the earth. Mental illness and addiction don't evidence themselves. No rules will be broken. Death, abuse, divorce: none of these. No revenge is exacted. No combat. You might argue that the hidden conflict is any resistance society might place upon this story, attacking what is being presented as calm, peaceful, serene, and finding its faults, insisting it must be more complicated, that something this complex cannot be executed so simply, but you will not see any of that here. The people in this story surround themselves with those who accept and nurture them. They have found little to no resistance locating people to place into their most intimate primary and secondary circles. There is no obstacle that requires overcoming. This is not the story of love being stronger than social mores or broken tradition. This is not a morality tale about the goodness of one character triumphing over the bad of another.

I pick up my sons from day care. They have this recurring vim that astonishes me daily. Everything about them is emphatic, nothing implicit. I like their boldness, their volume, their exaggeration. We make dinner together. They are small and it is impossible to find fault with their vigor, but I try to let them use their power to punish the greens for the salad and make the most of their curiosity by simplifying the onions into only their most useful layers. My husband arrives home and he offers perky slips of his hand across my back and brazen sentiments of perfection to the children. They hoot and cheer him on like he is their man in the fighting pits. He steals my workforce to usher them outside to burn off energy so they will calm at the table. When they return, the meal is ready. He gets the children settled and meets me in the kitchen as I'm grabbing the last dish. He rolls his full lips across mine and allows his tongue to slip through. I could nearly drop the platter I'm holding. "Good day at work?" he asks, and I nod, stealing another kiss from him before slapping his ass to get him moving.

Essay we now a somewhat loftier task!

At bath time, I supervise as my sons wash themselves. I am needed only as a referee and to swoop in with a dry towel if someone bumps his head or gets soap in his eyes. I lean in to kiss their brows when it is time to shut off the light. This is my second-favorite smell.

With a new breed of men sent down from heaven.

After the boys go to sleep, we set to our evening tasks: folding laundry, cleaning up the kitchen, taking out the trash, sorting the mail, and addressing items that need attention. I shepherd my husband through the golden work of nature, acts of encounter and romance. I pluck flowers from the gardens of his nerves and conflict his sense of urgency and tranquility.

The lip of it is hanged about with curling ivy, ivy freaked with a cassidony which goes twisting and twining among the leaves in the pride of her saffron fruitage.

It is a rustic fantasy we live out here in the suburbs. The days morph to nights and back into days. The calendar appears to exist only for those who refuse to live in the silver ideal of the instant. In our little locus amoenus, we revel in the undemanding abandon of passion and tradition and harmony. We hear the falling melodies and remind ourselves they are just an imitation. If those feelings of happiness pass, then so, too, will this sorrow. We speak with an elated eloquence: accidental fables, prestigious madness, worthy joy, happy detachment. We compose our mirth. We trespass the shadows. We bind simplicity to our pleasures. It is a human emphasis we place on the gods we construct.

And, see, the farm-roof chimneys smoke afar

You have been waiting for the threat. That is where you are wrong.

LOSER

I DIDN'T HAVE A SINGLE FRIEND TO LEAVE
behind. The whole school envied these girls, but everyone
else already had friends, and the risk of moving from one
group to another was too great. I didn't suffer such a conun-
drum. When I tried to think about what type of person I
was, I drew a blank, and so I wondered if I could stretch and
braid that nothing into a form they might welcome. If I
found success, only my loneliness would require an apology.
I registered a current of magic speeding beneath their skin,
and I wanted more than anything to know if that spurred

pulse was stoked by sinister power or innocent wiles. Most likely it was some bewitching balance of the two.

I was pale, but well rested, so I glowed in a way that required making up in other, lesser complexions. I liked chunky sweaters and dark jeans and classic sneakers, none of which provided any indication as to a personality. I wasn't quick to react, which allowed for a level of mystery. Perhaps it was this same combination of qualities that prevented others from trying to befriend me. They assumed I had my own people or they couldn't tell if I was like them and so they didn't engage.

I had a plan. I spent hours in a department store, on countless days, sniffing cardboard strips of paper trying to figure out what scent it was the lot of them wore, until my nose no longer registered the differences, burned by the deep inhales of alcohol. I returned many times to continue, marking possibilities in a notebook, leaning forward in chemistry class to smell the backs of necks to check my work. When I finally figured out which bottle held the answer, I begged my mother to buy it for me.

"You'll have to pay for that yourself," she said.

I had just started working at a bakery. I'd planned to save the money for college, but one purchase to celebrate the beginning of my employed life seemed reasonable. I'd save every other penny. When I received my first paycheck I took the bus to the mall and laid my cash down on the counter. The saleswoman handed me the bottle in a box wrapped in tissue and dropped in a bag. It all felt like ceremony appropriate to the gravity of my endeavor. Before I left, I sprayed myself once with the tester. It seemed economical. I'd keep a tally of how many sprays the bottle held so I could work out how many cents I spent a day.

The next morning I blew my hair dry. It looked exactly the same, but making the effort caused an internal change. I applied mascara and lip gloss. I felt the same things I had as a kid when a tooth loosened: a shiver of potential and a safe sort of danger. I couldn't stop tonguing that excitement. I spritzed myself with the bottle, felt a pang in my salivary glands.

In the locker room the next day, Angela saw me pull the perfume from my bag. I registered what I thought was an affliction of privilege take over her face. "What's that?" she asked. I'd anticipated her seeing me spray the perfume, smelling her own scent, and feeling her acceptance of me triggered.

"Rogue," I said. "Would you like to smell it?" If I pretended I didn't know it was what she wore, it wouldn't appear like the desperate bid for friendship it was.

"I can smell it from here." She slammed her locker door and the bank of metal quivered. "Putrid." Her smile appeared almost kind.

Tears stung my eyes and I put the bottle back in my purse. I thought of saying, *It's your scent. I know it is*, but I stopped myself, afraid my embarrassment might blossom on my cheeks. Her shoulder brushed mine as she walked out.

In chemistry, Tina turned and sniffed. "Is there something rotting in here?" Everyone else glanced around, confused. "Elaine, is that you?"

"I don't think so," I said.

"Are you wearing perfume?" she asked.

"Yes," I said, my eyes loading themselves again.

"It's not right," Tina said.

"It's Rogue," I responded, and I knew that naming the scent as a defense showed my hand.

"I've always hated that scent," she said. "Can you skip it tomorrow? I can't concentrate with a headache."

I refused to slump in my chair. Samantha, a mathlete, also excluded from that band of elites, flashed skepticism at Tina, and then transformed it to disappointment when her eyes shifted to me. She understood what Tina was denying me, and she thought less of me for wanting it.

On the bus home, Bella leaned across the aisle, placed her hand on my neck, and whispered in my ear, "I think someone on the bus is wearing Rogue. I could just throw up." She'd never spoken to me before.

"Who are you?" I asked.

She tilted her head and squinted, pulling away.

At my stop, I left the bottle on the seat. As the bus drove

off, I saw Bella slide over and hold the bottle to her nose, then spray herself.

I walked home, surprised I didn't feel more disappointed. Maybe I'd known the plan would never work. I'd wash my sweater that night, erase every trace of this effort.

In the kitchen, my mother asked if she could smell the perfume that I'd wasted my money on.

I told her I'd already lost it.

Her wooden spoon clattered against the pan as she turned to me. "Already?"

"What's the opposite of losing?" I asked. Was it winning or finding? In either case, the answer was yes.

THE HALIFAX SLASHER

HOW ANGRY COULD SUZY HAVE BEEN IF SHE poured me a drink after packing my bags? I couldn't help wondering if she was telling me the truth. We sipped on our brandies and she said I'd have to go. She'd kept me around in the hopes I could protect her, but if such dangers hadn't been prevented with me here, there wasn't a need for me to stay. All of it seemed a bit too easy.

"Where will you go?" Suzy asked me, like I could have an answer to that already. She asked if I wanted her to make me a couple sandwiches to sustain me, and I nodded like it was the least she could do.

I listened to her rustle about in the kitchen, and looked at the clutter left behind by the previous evening. The sideboard looked blank without the heavy, sculpted candlesticks. The contents of the cabinets below still spilled among the legs of the dining room table. I righted the armchair and wondered at what a thief, in his hurry, would want with toppling a big piece of furniture like that, thought of what kind of struggle must have occurred.

Suzy returned with a cube of wax paper—two sandwiches stacked and wrapped for traveling. She held them out and when I didn't take them from her, she set them on the table in front of me. I studied her face, the heavy, ashy swelling around her left eye, the scabbed welt of her bottom lip, the thin bruising around her neck. Even in all my anger, I was overcome with the prayer that she would come through all of this without the scar of fear, without the sharp swoop of a broken bone interrupting the smooth landscape of her features.

"Suzy, you're in shock. You shouldn't make drastic decisions just after something like this has happened. Let's give it a couple weeks. If you still feel this way, I'll leave, but forcing me out doesn't gain you control, and I don't think it's what you really want." I took her hand and pulled her down to the couch. Her face was frozen, unbroken by my plea. In truth, her demeanor had not changed since the attack. She was a solid woman, sure of her decisions, drastic in their execution. I'd feared this day since the moment I'd lit her cigarette at the train station. She was the sort who would throw herself from a sea cliff, and mean it. We'd all nod in understanding when we heard, knowing regret wasn't in her emotional repertoire.

"I'll never know how I'd feel differently if you'd been here with me, but you weren't. You're gone most of the time. I need to protect myself." Her eyes snarled, but in them I didn't see hurt; I saw contempt, an eagerness for me to get gone.

A hard slice of spring wind broke under the door, heralding someone in the entry. We looked in the direction of the hall and listened as the tight steps of the dancer ascended the stairs, paused halfway up, continued, accompanied by a sweet, slow whistle.

When we heard the door close above us, Suzy stood and retrieved my jacket from the coatrack. "Go."

"I'll sleep on the sofa. At least let me get this sorted." I felt alert, like all of my wires had been pulled taut. I suddenly couldn't imagine how I'd paint this for Paul. I couldn't fathom the sloppy humility I'd need to muster to explain why I was at his house in need of a place to stay.

She grumbled. "One night will turn into a week. You leave now and we're done with it. I'm not a lunatic, Henry. What happened was just the last straw in a situation that's been mounting a long time. I won't beg. I know you'll do what I ask." She turned from me and knelt at the sideboard to return the table linens to the drawer. She examined a slender piece of china for chips and set it carefully back on the shelf.

I felt the sunken fullness of relenting. My feet weighted me down, providing leverage to stand, and, once up, dragging me to the door. "I'll be at Paul's if you need anything."

"I know and I won't," she said without turning her head. I waited for a last look, for a glimpse I could hold in my mind and analyze on the walk across town, but she kept this from me.

It wasn't twenty-four hours before Paul passed me the afternoon paper. "Look at this." On the front page was another story of the man who'd attacked Suzy. It took only a moment to realize why the building looked so familiar. I glanced at Paul, confused. "He visited the same place two nights in a row?" Paul shrugged. I read as quickly as I could, my eyes tripping down the page, until I got to the line, "27-year-old dancer, Karolina Benecky."

"It says she found the thief in her closet upon returning home at ten p.m., but we heard her come in. We didn't hear anything above us. No scream, no struggle. And we would have heard someone leave. Could he have been hiding all that time?"

"Did they catch him?" Paul browsed the other sections of the newspaper.

"No, it says he had a knife this time and tried to slash at the girl's throat, but she raised her hands, and he put a gash in her palm and fled the scene."

"That's it? Lucky Karolina. Could have been much worse, eh?"

"She's a dancer, though. It says a tendon was severed permanently. That's unfortunate."

"Sure, but how long would that career have lasted anyway?" Paul was logical to a fault. His stony lack of empathy targeted the weak and the creatively inclined.

"I'm sure Suzy would never admit it, but she must be startled."

Paul looked up at me and shook his head. "She's not your ward anymore. The sooner you move on, the better."

I brushed this off. My feelings could not change immediately. I believed the situation still might reverse itself.

It was after this that the assaults started accumulating.

The attacker's rage surprised some girl by slicing her undressed shoulders. The police who arrived at the scene were barely able to decipher the words through her fragile breath.

Another woman, found unconscious and bruised, said the slasher accosted her like a cloud of stones, punching her head and knocking her about, brandishing a knife, but never using it.

The fifth victim, shuffling down an alley, humming to herself, heard another voice accompanying her own. She tried to flee, but ran the wrong way toward a bricked dead end. She was cut and bandied about. A neighbor noticed her emerging from the alley, rushed the window open to ask if she was all right, taking her in to call the authorities.

A heroic drunk was damaged by a force he said he

couldn't rightly recognize. From looking at the photo in the newspaper, I could see it was the years of neglect that had done him the greatest harm, but the reporter braided his story into the list of the others like a notable anomaly, like one more strand in the building case.

The town was up in arms. Women at the market whispered about how it was beginning to feel like a different place. People became reluctant to pull their curtains open in the morning. Families out for a stroll glanced behind them, looking for a knowing security, but feeling their heart rates rise even at the sight of an old friend, wondering, "Could Tom be the one?"

A woman turned up with the lining of her dress torn down, her calves gouged with deep wounds; she said the man had emerged from under a wooden platform set up in the middle of town. She'd stopped on her way home to eat an apple and look at the stars. She chastised herself for lingering, blamed herself for collapsing on an out-of-date sense of safety.

The eighth victim was held down under a man's soft grunts. She claimed she'd surrendered, worried about an unknown worst case. Her fear blurred in a flutter around her, her unmarred skin a backward sort of proof of the trauma she'd suffered.

A mob attacked a man they thought to be the slasher. On the crowded boardwalk, a woman believed she was being followed. She turned abruptly and screamed that she would not fall as his next victim and began boxing the man about the ears with her purse and umbrella. The man, startled, any memory of what she could be referring to knocked out of him, tried to push her away, and soon the onlookers involved themselves. One man held the supposed slasher down while another pummeled his face and gut. The slasher called out that he was trying to get home from work, that he didn't know what they were talking about, and when police finally appeared to break up the fight, it became apparent that the man was no slasher at all. The woman who'd made the accusation refused to turn over her resolve. "I will not be a victim. All men should give women their distance."

On the sixth day, two people showed up at the police station separately. They took them in one by one. The first was the third victim who'd had her bare shoulders sliced by the assailant. She'd returned to share more information. She fumbled about with her hands, a species of guilt creeping across her face, and then she named it plain. "I made up my attack," she said. "There wasn't a bit of truth to it. I did it for the attention. I'm having trouble at work, and I thought my boss might cut me a bit of slack." The two officers in the room looked at each other and leaned in. "That's a rotten thing to do, but set aside your shame for a moment and tell us more." She explained that she used her manicure scissors to make the slashes, and then screamed for someone to help her. It was simple enough. "And why are you coming forward?" they asked. The ugly inspiration loosed itself, and a look of innocence washed into her affect. "I believe others could be doing the same."

The police brought in the second woman to hear her story. She sobbed so hard her teeth shook inside her mouth. When the officers pressed her on every detail, she pushed back. "Why are you being so cruel? It's not as if I wanted this to happen." But the police looked at the story and its perfectly smooth details and felt the urge to crack it wide open. They waited for her to heave out the facts, all the while wondering if they were wrong, until finally, after begging for a glass of water, she broke out her bitter truth. "Fine," she said. "I made it up. I cut myself and wanted that panicked attention my family would pay me."

It was after this story came out in the papers that the attacks stopped. "Halifax Slasher Victims 3 & 9 a Hoax!" The young women consented to having their photographs on the front page and took interviews.

I thought of Suzy and how she must feel that someone had imitated her misfortune. No doubt, she'd feel an ounce of pride. Her shoulders would roll back knowing she had felt the truth of such fear. She'd scoff at a person who'd once harbored commitment, disappearing through the trapdoor of her own story. *Weak*, she'd think.

The police checked in with the other victims after these false accusations, and one by one they confessed that they didn't have the details to support their stories, either. "Mass

Hysteria," the next headline said. "A Town Out of Its Mind with Fear ... or Opportunity?"

When only Suzy and Karolina were left unconfessed, the police called them in. They interrogated them for hours, asking for details from them separately. They asked the women to identify the assailant in a lineup, asked them to pick out the slasher from a stack of photos they flashed one by one. There were discrepancies in how the two women described the man, but not enough that it was impossible it might have been the same suspect. Both women claimed their homes had been dark. Both women stuck to the story of not having gotten a good look at him. Both women mentioned the gold buckles on the man's shoes flashing in the light from the window.

On this afternoon, a third person showed up at the station: a man claiming to be the slasher. The police eyed him skeptically, but took his confession.

They put him in a lineup, and still the women closed their eyes and shook their heads, disappointed. The officers questioned the man who'd confessed and found enough errors that it couldn't be him. "Why are you lying?" the cops asked, but the man wouldn't give up.

The police informed the women that they had someone who'd confessed to the crimes, and the women both paused. They looked at the officers with disbelief, and nodded without saying a word.

Then: "Can I see him?" Suzy said.

Then: "What does he look like?" Karolina asked, a room away.

"You've already seen him," each officer said. "He was in the lineup."

It was then that Karolina began to cry. It was then that Suzy repeated, "Like I said, it was dark."

The police listened as Karolina told them that it was all made up.

The police glared at Suzy, daring her to stick to her story.

The police fixed on the false confessor, full of black-eyed boldness and certainty. The police listed out for him all the details he got wrong, watched the man's fury grow. The police warned him that falsely confessing was a punishable offense. They asked him, "Why?" The man appeared confused, insisted the attacks were his fault, but then crumbled, wondering if the officers could be right. Could he be mistaken? Could he not have done it after all? He couldn't think. One officer looked at the other, and then said to the man, "You'll need to get your head on straight." The man nodded, convinced.

The police stared at Suzy, waiting for the moment they could tell her she was lying.

Suzy thought of all that fear she'd created. She thought about the state of upheaval she'd set upon the town. She touched the scab on her lip, and felt nothing but truth.

BULL'S-EYE

PHYLLIS LAID OUT THE LUCKY CHARMS BEFORE
her: the green mini–Beanie Baby bear, the purple mini–
Beanie Baby bear (released in commemoration of Princess
Diana's death), the statue of the Virgin Mary that had been
her mother's, the small strand of jingle bells, and the spider
toy she'd watched her upstairs neighbor, the young boy,
playing with on the front stoop before carelessly leaving it
behind when his mother took him up for dinner.

She felt a pang of guilt looking at the spider, but then remembered it was that same little boy who kept her awake

as he stomped around heavy-soled and monstrous. Even on the quiet nights—the nights when she couldn't hear a single sign of life above her—she stared at the dim ceiling, praying and telling herself not to think about the possibility that the footsteps and high-pitched whining could start at any moment. The anxiety was enough to keep her up until it was nearly light out.

Phyllis had purchased the minimum number of bingo cards, which still seemed like a heck of a lot to her. Eighteen cards on a single sheet. She pulled out her bright blue dauber and got to work on filling out the bulk of the coverall numbers she saw already up on the board. Phyllis sat alone, in front of the women she'd dubbed Henny and Penny. Henny and Penny talked nonstop, narrated every little thing that happened. Henny made a soft cooing noise every time she stamped her dauber down, and Penny spoke the name of the most recently called number aloud like it was the most interesting thing she'd ever heard.

At the table beside her sat Carlo and his mother-in-law, Bette. Carlo had rented one of the computers with 144 cards. Phyllis thought the computers took the fun out of the game. *When was the last time I saw someone win without a computer?* She tried to force herself not to think about it. She was on a strict budget and the $15 for the 18-On pack was all she could afford. *It's more about the fun and anticipation than the winning,* she told herself, though wouldn't it be nice if just once she got a return on her investment? *Computers*, she thought, *are basically cheating*. Only the true gamblers paid for a computer, like the women at the riverboat who pressed the button on the slot machine instead of pulling the lever, so anxious for the rush they couldn't even bother to anticipate.

Phyllis waited for this night every week. She slogged through her schedule of television shows each evening, drifting off more often than not, left to dream about the resolution of each episode. Thursday nights, though, represented the climax of the week. Getting on the bus down to the bingo hall caused a particular sense of eager freedom to rush through her. As she descended the stairs into the fluorescent church basement, the humid, artificial air-conditioning felt at once comforting and disappointing. As she walked through the double doors, she'd glance around at the people already there, seeing them for the sad and lonely individuals they were, but only in flashes. Her eyes would focus in and out, feeling joy in the recognition that this was the best night of the week for many, and palpable anxiety that in the span of the next two hours the night would be over. The church basement was run-down, but she only noticed that for the first few moments. Like quickly adjusting to the smell of another person's home, she shifted from seeking out tiles that needed replacing and paint that needed touching up, and focused, instead, on the bright bingo board, displaying the

first of the numbers, already posted to keep the early
birds occupied.

The big tension of routine was what kept her coming back.
She had a bad heart, and she wondered about getting herself worked up, but a woman can only take so many milque-
toast evenings full of fill-in puzzles and word jumbles and
hour-long police procedurals. If this was the way she would
go, then so be it. Stanley had died years ago and she had
waited long enough to be with him again.

When they called the first winner, the applause was light.
A volunteer ran over, her apron full of pull-tabs, to look at
the screen of the woman's computer. People tore off the top
sheets of their packs and stuffed them into the trash bags
taped to their tables before the winner had even been confirmed; the computers were never wrong. Phyllis watched
as the player's friend nodded in approval at the win, unable
to muster any more enthusiasm than that.

Phyllis began daubing her free spaces on the next card. The
typical rustling that happened between games rose up, until
Phyllis felt a small thrill at seeing a number come up on the
monitor, unnoticed by others. She marked off her spaces and
quietly folded her hand around the small string of jingle
bells. When the caller finally sang out, "I-twenty-two," it was
Phyllis who led the charge with her bells. Phyllis felt the luck
rise in her. Twenty-two was her number and she would prove

it. If she won, she could avoid boiling down her options for an entire week. She might buy the nicer brand of decaf coffee at the store. She might treat herself to the full rack of ribs from the take-out place on the corner so that she'd have leftovers for lunch the next day. She might sift through the bin at the dollar store and pick out a new pearlescent-pink nail polish to cover the white, hard ridges that striated her nails.

Phyllis didn't need to focus when she was daubing her numbers. Her mind could wander. She could think of all of the fortune she'd had in her life, all the loving family that surrounded her, even if their visits fell few and far between. As the next bingo was called, she ripped off her top sheet and placed it into her trash bag. She remembered when she'd started coming to play, how she'd thought what a waste it was that each player had their own garbage bag, but it wasn't long before she'd blinded herself to this detail, too.

Her son: she missed. Alvin lived far out in the suburbs and had health problems of his own. He was mostly homebound, but he rarely answered the phone. She wondered who he thought he was fooling. Her grandson, Tip, in his early thirties, came to visit every couple weeks. He brought her a few items she couldn't round up in her neighborhood, and sometimes cookies from the Polish store or French crullers from the donut chain. She liked both equally in theory, but on a given day she always wished for one more than the other, and had trouble not letting him know if his offering didn't match up with her hope. When he visited, she always ended up running through her list of ailments, past and present. She rambled off the list of surgeries she'd had. She showed him her arthritic hands and rolled up her pant leg so he could see the swollen bulb of her knee. It was during these visits that she made up for the lost time of being alone for the better part of each day. She spoke nonstop for his two-hour visits. She had to; he was nearly silent. She wondered at how young people got by without the art of conversation. In her mind, a story retold trumped silence. The one where her grandson slipped on the droppings in the chicken run. The one where he said nonsensical things that turned out to be true and profound. The one where he would play with her best friend's son. Oh no, that must have been Alvin. Silly her. Now that he was grown, Tip reminded her so much of Alvin. Who could blame her for getting them confused?

Phyllis programmed her mind to the next version of the game, which was called Postage Stamp. Four numbers in a small square in any corner of a card. The numbers began appearing on the screen before they were called and she got to work. Very quickly, bingo was called at the table next to her. A young woman, *An amateur*, Phyllis thought silently, beamed and held up her card. Even with Phyllis's eyesight what it was, she could see it was a false call. The girl had a regular bingo, not the postage stamp she was supposed to be looking for. Phyllis shook her head and thought back to when she was just starting to play and she'd made a false call. It was embarrassing enough that it gave her an extra rush of adrenaline in future games: the pressure not to draw undue attention racing through her system as she double-checked her card before silently raising her hand.

She was equally embarrassed to call bingo when it was a legitimate winner; a sadness accompanied the motion of ending a particular game, a sense of letting the rest of the group down, taking away the private hope of the others in the room to bask in her own singular success, one game closer to the end of the night.

Phyllis daubed and let her mind drift to her home and how to empty it. She thought about what she could give to her grandson to make the space blanker and easier to clean. She remembered a three-tier cookie tray she could offer him to give to his girlfriend.

She clucked at Henny and Penny paying fifty cents for a small bowl of popcorn the volunteers popped on the cafeteria stovetop, and listened to them coo over it for the next three games. "Doesn't that just hit the spot?" Henny said, and, like clockwork, Penny responded, "Right on the nose. Isn't this a treat?"

Phyllis always felt a bit stunned by how quickly the evening broke up after the last bingo was called. She packed her dauber and lucky charms into the free tote she'd gotten from the library, and by the time she looked up, most everyone else had gone. She worked her way slowly to the door and up the wide stairs, one rise at a time.

The heavy doors were propped open, letting in the heat and the thick sound of cicadas weighing down the night. "Going so soon?" Don said. Don, in his polo shirt and ball cap, stood there all evening, every week. She smiled politely at Don and felt the urge to ask him if he knew her name. She felt the urge to ask him, *What is it you do here, exactly?* But instead she said, "I'll see you next week, then," and Don nodded once.

As she walked to the bus stop, she looked up at the dim sky, at the deep contrast of the power lines against it. She passed an alley and heard a rigid skittering, half hoping she'd see a rat, but found none. She passed a house where children still jumped about the yard, even at that hour, and didn't allow herself to wonder at how their parents were raising them.

On the bus, a young man careened wildly around, stumbling up to people, trying to make conversation. He bumped her shoulder and apologized, hollered up to the driver to learn how to drive, placing blame elsewhere for his own lack of control. As he passed, she said a prayer for the young man, and chided herself for feeling inconvenienced by his misfortune. She rang for her stop, and the bus driver wished her a good night. She waited for the hiss of air to indicate the bus had knelt itself down to deliver her more safely to the curb.

At her house, she opened the screen door and, on impulse, gave the rotten wood of her front door a swift kick, breaking through the bottom panel. She felt an immediate satisfaction. She locked the screen door and slept without fear.

The next day, while Phyllis waited for the handyman to come fix the door, her neighbor stopped by to bring tomatoes from her garden. They chatted on the front porch for a while, Phyllis wondering if she should invite her neighbor in, but worried about making her feel obligated to stay. They talked about the family across the street whose television had been stolen the week before, and the neighbor shook her head sadly. "I don't lock my door because of criminals and thieves. They'll find a way to get in no matter what," the neighbor said. "I lock my door because of good people faced with unexpected opportunity." Phyllis nodded, but inside she felt turned around. She tried to understand what her friend had said, but couldn't make it work.

She tuned out and looked up the street to see the upstairs tenant approaching, pushing her son in his stroller, passed out from the heat and excitement of a trip to the park. So gentle-looking compared to the monster she imagined bumping around above her each night. It was then Phyllis thought of his spider, the boy's toy she'd found and claimed as her own lucky charm. She thought of chance and opportunity, honesty and integrity. She thought of putting the spider back on the stoop for the boy to find later. She knew what could happen and what couldn't. For a moment she could see herself clearly, but just as quickly, she looked away.

HALF DOLLAR

After Shirley Jackson

I DIDN'T WANT PATTY TO SEE MY RELUCTANCE, but my conscience won out. "Patty, are we sure? This feels different. We'll be on someone else's turf."

I'd watched Patty walk out of department stores with sweaters, only to return them hours later for store credit. I'd allowed her to swap our ginger ales for pints of beer when the men at the tavern stood to take their turns in the darts games. Wandering into a stranger's yard without a plan, though, seemed more illicit.

Patty responded by pushing the gate open. She started down the path, which was covered in leaves and brush several seasons old. As soon as I stepped past the fence, all of the streetlamps went out. I looked back, and I could still see the iron constellation high above. The shine stopped at the deep shrubs lining the fence. I had trouble seeing as far as my feet and so I stepped gingerly, and clasped a hand on Patty's shoulder. Like always, I wanted to leach some of her assured energy.

Patty shrugged me off, saying, "Get. You're not afraid, are you?"

I shook my head, relieved she hadn't seen me lie my cowardice away. When we reached the front porch, Patty's foot ripped a large creak from the first step. I jumped within, but inhaled, holding steady without.

Patty tilted down, to examine the wood of the step with her fingertips. "Soft, nearly rotted through," she said, turning to me. She straightened, and lifted herself easily up the next two stairs. A dim light shined behind the sheer. Patty stood in front of the door, measured, observant. I was too nervous to think of anything but what would happen next. After several seconds, I saw Patty's hand rise. I looked for a shadow, but the absence of light let her knuckles fall without a mark. She gave three quick raps, and clasped her hands behind her back, raising her head to look toward the small window at the top of the door.

In a moment, the fixture above us, bulb half clouded by dead bugs and grit, flicked on. We heard a chain lock slide and fall slack and a whoosh of air sucked into the house as the door eased back, like a vacuum opening.

Before us stood a woman, not thin so much as empty of herself. She had been fuller at some point, and in the once-filled spaces, a lack coaxed our attention. She didn't say a word, only looked behind us, searching for some other element of our arrival.

"Mrs. Pengrine?" Patty said, and I snapped my sight on her, wondering what sort of chance Patty was taking. The woman raised one eyebrow, and nodded her head as slowly as I've ever seen. "So nice to meet you, Mrs. Pengrine. I was wondering, is Mr. Pengrine home?"

Mrs. Pengrine breathed deeply, like that rush of air through the door, and shook her head.

Patty took this well. "All right, then, might I leave a message for him? It's very important."

It was then I saw the mailbox beside the door with MR. AND MRS. A. PENGRINE embossed in gold on the black matte. Patty was the most ghastly. I would never catch up.

The woman brought a hand to her mouth absently, rubbed her forefinger against her lips, stalling, like she didn't much care to speak the answer she had at the ready, but her hand dropped, and she had her say. "I'm afraid you can't. Mr. Pengrine is no longer with us."

Patty gulped air. We had practiced our gasps in front of the mirror, rehearsed their timing and strength, trying to make them as believable as possible. Patty played master and I apprentice, as usual. "That can't be," she said. "That just simply can't be."

Mrs. Pengrine stood stock-still, interested in Patty's

shock. Her face held skepticism, hope, defensiveness, threat, but she said nothing.

"Certainly you mean that Mr. Pengrine has moved away? Not that he's . . ." Patty acted as though she couldn't bring herself to say it.

"No, I'm afraid he's passed on. Six months ago now, may he rest."

Patty cast a glance my way, shock asking for confirmation, and I did my best to return it to her.

"But my friend and I, just this afternoon, we passed him at the station. He nearly stepped in front of a streetcar, and I pulled his arm back. He thanked me over and over. Said he was distracted, trying to find a gift for his wife."

Mrs. Pengrine's face remained stern, but her eyes filled. "You must have the wrong man. It couldn't have been my Arnold."

Patty shook her head, refusing to accept this answer. "It must have been. He said his name was Arnold Pengrine, and he said I should stop by this address anytime for a reward. He said he didn't have any cash on him, but if we stopped by this evening, he'd give us each a quarter and fresh-cut roses from the garden."

Mrs. Pengrine gazed past us to the front of the yard, and I realized Patty had noticed the thorny branches on the bushes. "Two quarters? That's hardly . . . and the roses aren't blooming this time of year," the woman said, like the fault lay in the flowers and not in the specter of her husband's promise.

"But how could we have seen him, if he's gone?" Patty asked the woman, like Mrs. Pengrine might have the answer, like Mrs. Pengrine ought to defend herself from this accusation.

I felt sick, like perhaps I'd had enough. "Patty," I whispered.

"Margaret, you saw him, too! How can this be?" Patty snapped.

I shook my head, wishing myself away from this front porch, wishing I had no part in this, wishing Patty wasn't so horrid.

"Would you come in? I'd love to hear more," Mrs. Pengrine said, stepping back to open a space in the doorway.

"I don't think we'd better," Patty said, taking my hand and turning us to leave. "Come on, Margaret."

"Girls, just a moment or two, we can sit on the porch here. I understand if you don't want—"

Before she could finish, Patty let out the slightest shriek, halting us in our steps. She let go of my hand to point, and there on the bottom step lay two quarters. I thought back to Patty stooping to touch the rotten wood, and knew it was then she'd placed the coins.

"I—I'm so sorry we've disturbed you, ma'am. We'll be on our way. Good night!" She grabbed my hand again, hopping past the last two steps. I stumbled behind her, but kept my grip. We slammed the gate behind us and raced for what felt like blocks.

"How"—Patty beamed at me—"was *that*?"

"Oh, Patty," I said. "The most ghastly. I don't know . . . That poor woman."

Patty pushed my shoulder roughly. "Oh, come on! We made her night. She thinks her husband's spirit is alive and well and visiting young girls. No harm done. What a miserable sight she was!" Patty collapsed on a bench, panting and laughing, doubled over.

"But how did you know to place the quarters? You used the rosebushes and the name on the mailbox. How did you know it would work out?" I felt hot and red-faced. I wondered if we'd missed our ride home.

"Of course I had no idea *how* it would work out! I just paid attention and followed the clues! Oh, we must do more! You'll need to take a turn, Margaret!"

I nodded. It was true. I knew. If we were to remain friends, I'd need to try to top her. I'd need to draw out some demons and swirl them around some unsuspecting mark. "It's probably time to meet your mother," I said.

Patty slid her watch below the sleeve of her coat and called out, "Cripes, you're right!"

We walked back to the corner of Nation and Main since Patty had left our streetcar fare on the steps, and all the way, Patty pointed to houses, dreaming up schemes. When we got to the corner, her mother was upset. "Where have you been? It's nearly half past!"

"Mother, you wouldn't believe! We saved a man's life! He almost stepped out in front of the streetcar, and I pulled him back! We're heroes!"

I marveled at Patty's ability to turn her first lie so believably inside out into a second.

"Well, la-di-da," Patty's mother said, unimpressed. "Next time you save someone's life, be back on time."

Patty just laughed and hooked her arm in mine as we walked to her mother's car. Her elbow dug lightly into my ribs, and she whispered, "You're next, Margaret."

My heart stopped, thinking she meant I'd be her next mark, but in a moment I realized she meant the next prank was mine to perform. I clutched her arm tighter, and wondered at how my mind had looked first for the threat in what she'd said, and doubt fell over where it was I should have laid my trust.

MANIFEST

BERNADETTE NEEDED A MOLE REMOVED FROM beside her left ear. The mole was of an ample enough size and prominent enough placement on her face that her dermatologist recommended she visit a plastic surgeon to ensure minimal scarring. The doctor said he could provide her with a referral but Bernadette's PPO would certainly cover just about anyone.

Bernadette eyed her doctor, looking for an indication of how the young man might possibly hold within his head both the proper treatment of all skin maladies and the networks of each of his patients' insurance policies. She could find no such evidence. And anyway, she had only one recollection of a friend visiting a plastic surgeon in the past—a high school acquaintance who had talked her parents into paying for a tummy tuck so slight that Bernadette had been unable to tell the difference after the procedure, and while such a quality—not being able to notice evidence of the work done at all—might seem to endorse a doctor in a situation where the primary goal was a lack of scarring, Bernadette worried she might awake from the twilight sleep of surgery to find the mole still in place and a doctor insisting he'd completed his task. She would not trouble herself to track down her old high school friend for the doctor's name.

Bernadette was not a vain woman. She had no particular anxiety about being seen as less than perfect. Her complexion hummed with a sallow pallor that she refused to gussy up with foundation or blush. Her hair had once been a bright blond, but time and lack of sunlight had dulled its radiance. She found herself, at age thirty-five, still slim, but gathering the thin-skinned bladders of fat along her inner thighs and lower belly and triceps that she associated with her junior high teachers: women who had chalked the same basic algebra equations and timelines of historical events onto blackboards for decades, who wore the same dresses in which they'd begun teaching, increasingly ill-fitting as their bodies showed the evidence of babies born and hours spent each day commuting from the far-out suburbs they could afford. Bernadette recognized all of these similarities with a frustrated indignation, but did little to redirect her plot. Her weight stayed steady, but where lean muscle had previously made itself invisible, there existed now pocked bulges that she fondled and wagged a dozen times in the mirror before forgetting about them entirely.

On the day of the initial consultation, she navigated the anonymous halls of the office building until she arrived at the correct room: 215. The name appeared to be missing from the plastic sleeve below the number and so she paused outside to check again the card she'd been given by her primary care physician, confirming the location. When she'd called to make the appointment, the receptionist had kindly—though Bernadette thought unnecessarily, in this age of smartphones and GPS and Google Maps—offered to provide Bernadette directions. Outside of the unmarked office, Bernadette found herself regretting, for only a half second, not having taken them. If at all possible, Bernadette availed herself of all advice offered to her. She used this guidance to fend off criticism and failure. If someone happened to insult her or she missed a goal, she had only to call up the suggestions forced on her to explain away her deficiency and absolve herself of responsibility. It was a habit she recognized in herself occasionally, when wondering if she, as a human being, should display more accountability in her life, but each time, she quickly resolved the issue by stroking her self-inquisition into submission. Bernadette had read an article in *Time* about North Korean women who gathered weekly to perform "self-criticism," admitting their errors and faults to one another, not as a way of unburdening themselves of their worry, but as a sort of radical humility, destabilizing their status among the other women and encouraging themselves to be better the following week. Bernadette threw the magazine across the room. She could tell when something had gone too far, and she picked up her *Ladies' Home Journal* instead. Over and over, in women's magazines, she read that females were too hard on themselves. Ladies had a habit of expecting each aspect of their lives to be flawless and impeccable, and they could all benefit from "going a bit easier on themselves." It was with this strange circular logic that Bernadette used anonymous advice from a claptrap *Good Housekeeping* article to tell herself it was fine to eschew ownership of her own life and blame the counsel of others for her shortcomings. If Bernadette had accepted the directions of the receptionist, and this ended up being the wrong office, she could have placed blame on that helpful but idiotic woman. She had, this time, loosened from her code, and insisted she could find her own way.

Bernadette pushed open the door, a motion as close to stepping from Dorothy's gray tornado-tumbled house into Technicolor Oz as Bernadette had ever experienced. If the hall had been neutral and discreet, the waiting room of this plastic surgeon's office had the glowing aura of a recent nuclear meltdown. Bernadette's eyes stung with the mist of fake tanner and baby oil that invaded from all sides. She spied a middle-aged woman whose edges were so puffed and softened that she appeared as though she hovered behind a Vaseline-coated lens. A younger woman flipped idly through an *Us Weekly* resting below flesh stretched to its absolute limit. Bernadette could see the outline of gauze squares between the woman's nipples and her tank top. She wondered what offending ooze the medical padding was protecting. She sought refuge in the drooped melt of a burn victim's eye. She smiled weakly, relieved to find someone who had *need* of being in this place, and looked away to find the receptionist waiting behind her desk. Surprisingly, the woman looked absolutely natural. Bernadette assigned the woman more than her standard-issue assumption of integrity, granting that the woman was strong-willed enough not to fall prey to the warped standards of beauty that confronted her on a daily basis.

"Checking in?" the woman asked.

"I am. Bernadette Thomas to see Dr. Hoffman."

"Yes, of course, Ms. Thomas. Can I see your insurance card and your ID, please? You can start by filling these out. The final forms are a nondisclosure agreement. You can't mention anything you hear or see in this office outside of issues of your own care. I'll need you to initial each page and sign and date here. Any questions?" The receptionist flipped back to the top sheet and handed Bernadette the clipboard. Bernadette dug out her identification, and set to work.

Bernadette never knew how much to include or not on these forms when they asked about health history. In the space marked *Allergies*, should she mention that she was *sometimes* allergic to cats, in that if she petted someone else's cat and then touched her eyes, they would itch until she forced herself to just sleep off the irritation? In the space marked *Other*, should she note that she was prone to yeast infections? She omitted both of these details, but resolved to bring them up if the doctor asked a question that indicated either piece of information might be somehow relevant.

Before signing the NDA, she took a long, slow look around the room to acknowledge what she was signing away her right to talk about. One woman in the corner tended to a child beside her, both with wide, thick-hided noses, and Bernadette wondered if they were here to address that or if one of them might have a secret malady that required cosmetic attention: a lumpy deposit somewhere that would become visible in a warmer month, or a vestigial tail perched at the top of the child's butt crack.

Bernadette turned in the paperwork. The receptionist said something noncommittal about the wait. Bernadette clutched her purse in her lap. She surveyed the selection of magazines: *Allure, Golf, Money*. Bernadette was interested in none of them, and so she eyed the plastic rack of rainbow-colored pamphlets across the room instead. She wondered at whether the colors bore any relation to the content. Was the celadon of the *Micro Dermabrasion* pamphlet meant to denote cleanliness? Was the cornflower of the *Cellulite Treatments* pamphlet chosen for the cool serenity that might replace your bodily insecurity once you'd finally addressed those pesky bumps? Certainly the purple of the *Botox* pamphlet was a brand specification. Was the pale yellow of the *Liposuction* pamphlet supposed to remind you of the off-color fat lingering inside of you? The hot magenta color of the *Buttock Augmentation* leaflet seemed almost gaudy compared with the pale options flanking it. *Otoplasty?* Bernadette thought. She'd never heard of that one, and from looking at the picture of the smiling child on the front, she couldn't quite figure out what it was for.

A nurse emerged from the door beside the reception desk and said, looking up from her clipboard, "Bernadette?" Bernadette stood, pleased she had been called despite having been the last to arrive. The large-breasted woman stood as well, and they both halted, sharing a confused look before turning their eyes to the nurse. The nurse glanced down at her chart, and then at both women's chests. "Sorry about that! Bernadette Capirini." The other woman stepped forward. "What are the odds?" Bernadette heard the nurse say behind the door.

Bernadette sat wondering about her nominal counterpart, wondering if everything was all right with her implants or if she was the sort of person who decided to address issue after issue.

Bernadette caught the child staring at her and forced a smile, hoping to urge the child's eyes away, but they stuck in place. Bernadette wondered why the child didn't stare at the puffed lady or the burn victim. She wondered if the mother might reprimand him if he had. Because Bernadette looked like any other person, the mother let the staring go on without note. Bernadette decided this was wrong. No one should be stared at, disfigured or not. "Ma'am, I'd like to suggest that you tell your son not to stare at people that appear different from him."

The woman looked at Bernadette, confused, and then her eyes circled the room scanning the other patients. "Excuse me?" she asked.

"Your son was staring directly at me, and I think it's rather rude. Just because I am disfigured does not mean he has permission to stare." Bernadette felt a sick power wash through her, uncertain of what would happen next. She could tell the woman was flummoxed. The woman searched Bernadette, skimming her for the mutilation she might be referencing, and then giving up. "I'm very sorry. I'm sure he didn't mean to." She searched through her bag then, producing a picture book she handed to her son. "Tommy, why don't you read this?" Tommy accepted the book, but looked up at his mother. "What is *disfigured*?" The mother paused. "It's someone who has had an accident and looks different because of it." She glanced at Bernadette and smiled weakly, hoping her explanation was satisfactory. Tommy turned to Bernadette then. "You had an accident? What was it?"

Bernadette could have felt caught, but instead she looked straight ahead, sighed, and refused to answer.

One by one, Bernadette watched as the other patients

were called into the exam rooms. She kept willing another specimen to come through the waiting room door so she might examine them, and finally someone did: a handsome man whose features didn't appear to be amplified in any artificial way. She aimed her face slightly away from him and guided her peripheral vision in his direction as he filled out his paperwork.

After he turned in his clipboard, he sat back and looked directly at Bernadette. "Mole removal?" Bernadette was shocked and failed to respond at all for several moments. She would never have dreamed of asking someone why they were in any doctor's office. There was simply no protocol for it being done in a polite way because it was never the business of another. But how could he have known her reason for being there?

"I'm not comfortable talking about it, and I think it rather untoward of you to ask," Bernadette said. She looked away, but the man still gazed at her. He had movie-star good looks. About her age, but groomed well, confident, slim, and tan. He sat with his legs splayed casual and wide. He leaned his artfully shaped head of hair on the wall behind him.

This was the type of man Bernadette usually felt comfortable talking to, so far out of her league that she knew there was no threat of awkward tension, so attractive she found it hard to look at him. In a graph charting the uncanny valley, he was closer to the placement of a molded-rubber mannequin than he was to a real human being with wrinkles and blemishes. He was pretty, and she didn't usually find this quality appealing.

"Sorry! Didn't mean to pry," he said with a smirk.

Bernadette wanted to say, *Why are* you *here?* but she couldn't bring herself to be so petty, to ask for something she was unwilling to offer. Was it so hard to imagine that she might be getting an eye lift or butt augmentation? Was it a compliment that he looked at her and saw no obvious way her face could be improved, or was it clear that she was so far from caring about how she looked that no medically unnecessary procedure was even a possibility? Was the plastic surgery office for the ugly? Or might it be for the beautiful ones, the ones who were so close to perfect that they tried to tip over into that state of flawlessness, often overshooting it?

Bernadette had read enough tabloid headlines in the grocery store to know that once you started down the cosmetic procedure route, there was no stopping, for work of this sort did not age well. The re-forming and tightening and injecting served only to cause faces and bodies to warp and drag in more unnatural ways, so that one needed to continue returning to the office for more and more maintenance procedures until it was difficult to reconcile the slight improvement that was initially made with the constant compromise of each following treatment. Eyes disappeared to mere circles in one's head, mouth an immovable grimace, skin wan from chemical peels when not coated in bronzer.

When another nurse emerged to call her name, Bernadette could see immediately all of the office procedures this woman had sustained. She smiled at Bernadette, but her face did not wrinkle and her eyes did not move.

"See ya, Bernadette," the man said casually, like it was his right to know her name and use it. Bernadette glared at him, and couldn't shake her annoyance at his unearned familiarity.

Bernadette met with the doctor. She made an appointment to return for the procedure. She observed the newly occupied waiting room as she left, but the pretty man was gone.

Bernadette went home and read her advice columns, not for the advice, but to linger in the pity she felt for the people feeling the need to ask for it.

Bernadette listened to her answering machine. She had one message from a charity that called her at least twice a week. Somehow it worked out that she was never home for these calls. If she were, she would pick up the phone and ask them to stop calling, but in the meantime, she spent seconds identifying the message and deleting it only once it reached its end.

Bernadette marked the date of the surgery on the calendar on her fridge. She had picked the date because she had no plans immediately following it. Her social obligations dropped off the night before the surgery, so that afterward she could sequester her bandaged self until the wound had healed. It was not vanity she worried about post-operation, but rather the inevitable questions and obligatory concern she sought to avoid. She looked at those white, square days following the surgery and felt no trepidation.

Bernadette thought of the man from the waiting room. She sat down at her kitchen table and picked up a pen. She began to draw him on the back of an envelope. She was no artist. What she drew was little better than what a child might do. His eyes were at the top of his head. His mouth stretched nearly to the edges of his face. She had no idea how to re-create the swoop and start of his hair, and drew more lines than such a caricature required. When she finished, she placed the picture on her fridge with a realty magnet that had been stuck to her mailbox outside. The realty magnet showed the face of a blond woman in a suit, and Bernadette didn't like the way the placement suggested that the drawing of the man from the doctor's office knew the realtor, that they might be together, so she swapped in a giraffe magnet that was currently holding down a coupon for toilet paper, and gazed at her work, satisfied. There were three faces on the fridge now: the newly drawn portrait, the realtor magnet, and her niece's school picture. She made eye contact with all three and then went about her regular evening business.

In the following weeks before the surgery, Bernadette had dinner with a friend she found insufferable. The friend talked and talked, providing more detail on everything than was necessary. It wasn't as if Bernadette had anything to say, but still she silently critiqued her friend's inability to tell a concise and well-paced story. Bernadette wondered why she'd accepted the invitation. She rarely enjoyed these meals, but she knew, if asked again, she would accompany her friend to another appropriately budget-conscious meal. This evening they dined at a BYO Lebanese restaurant, and Bernadette ordered the chicken shawarma, while her friend ordered the falafel. Bernadette scrunched her nose, thinking it was the trendy thing to order and wondering how anyone could think falafel tastier than chicken or beef or lamb.

The waiter at the restaurant seemed distracted. He kept craning his neck back to check something in the kitchen, fumbling for a pen in his apron too long, asking them to repeat their order, ignoring their request for hot sauce, and ceasing to check in at all after delivering their meals, so that Bernadette had to listen to her friend for far longer than she intended to, lasering her eyes into the back of the restaurant to try to find someone, anyone, to rescue her.

When the check finally came, her friend said, "I've just been going on and on, but tell me! What's happening with you? What's new?"

Bernadette forced a small smile. "Not much! You know, same old, same old." She was not trying to blow off her friend's request. She could not think of anything worthy to tell her. The operation occupied her mind for a moment, but Bernadette decided not to mention it. It felt melodramatic to call it an "operation." For a brief second she considered saying something bold, like, *I'm getting plastic surgery!* but her mind was already three steps ahead. The joke was not that good. Her friend would express horror and then concern and then amusement. Bernadette could see it all unfold so clearly that she opted not to mention it at all.

At home that night, Bernadette tried to read her book for a while, a historical fiction that painted romance and intrigue in the court of French royalty. She couldn't get into it, though. She mined a pen out of her purse, tucked beside her on the floor next to the bed, and set about drawing the waiter from the restaurant on an endpaper of her book. She drew his heavy brow and speckled in a five-o'clock shadow. She made his nose the same width all the way down and drew crude teeth between the lips that remained slightly parted the whole night. For his hair, she couldn't quite remember, but she imagined it was short, and drew abbreviated straight lines crisscrossing his head, the result most comparable to a mussed haystack. Bernadette ripped the page from her book and got out of bed. She tucked the picture she'd drawn under a different corner of the realtor's magnet. She looked into the eyes of the patient, her niece, the realtor, and the waiter.

On the bus home from work the next day, a woman was passing out flyers for a young boy who'd gone missing. Severely autistic, he'd run out the open bus door before his mother could haul him back. Bernadette knew, as soon as her hand closed around the picture, that the boy belonged on the fridge as well. On her walk from the bus, Bernadette saw a duplicate of the realty magnet still stuck to the fence mailbox of a house that wouldn't sell. It was cracked from weather damage, but Bernadette grabbed it, wondered if her action constituted theft, told herself she was cleaning up the neighborhood.

She added the boy to the fridge, alongside the duplicate realtor, tried to cover the duplicate realtor with a corner of her portrait of the waiter, but then decided that the realtor's twin having been added to the family of faces was a sign she belonged there. She stood, for what she felt to be a long time, looking first into the eyes of the handsome man, then her niece, then the first realtor, and, immediately after, the second realtor, then the waiter and the missing boy. In reality, this action filled only a few seconds, but Bernadette could feel a strange routine developing, and she told herself she must stop.

In the following week, Bernadette added several more faces to the fridge: a female model from a perfume ad, a headshot she grabbed from the bulletin board of a coworker's local theater production, the illustrated portrait of a new columnist in the newspaper. Her magnets were getting weak from the weight of what they were being asked to hold.

The day for the surgery approached, and Bernadette asked her brother to accompany her to the appointment. He acted put out by having to take a day off work, but he didn't make Bernadette say what they both knew: that he was the only one she could ask.

In the waiting room, she was too nervous to be aware of the cast of characters populating the office, but she caught her brother staring at a man whose face looked like it had been blown back by a sudden gust, and she elbowed him. She regretted her action when he responded, "What?" Everyone looked at them and she stared straight ahead, unable to cover for his rudeness.

Bernadette woke woozy from the procedure. She felt alert, but her brother kept laughing at her, which she knew meant she was being silly or slow to respond.

When he'd come to take her to the appointment, he asked if he could drive her car because he needed to get gas and he didn't want her to be late. She agreed. When they returned to her apartment, he considered leaving right away, but thought better of it when she fumbled with her keys at the lock. He took them from her, and opened the door easily. Bernadette felt embarrassed, but remembered the nurse telling her to accept help for the next few hours. She might *feel* fine, but it would take a while for her to return to full capacity.

Light-headed, she took a seat at the kitchen table and asked her brother if he'd pour her a glass of juice. When her brother reached toward the refrigerator door handle, he saw all the faces. "What's all this, Bern?"

Bernadette looked at him and shook her head. She

felt rounded off, like anything she said would be an approximation.

"Did you draw these?" he asked, gesturing to the handsome man, the waiter, a newer portrait of a street preacher, a college student she saw working in the window of the coffee shop she passed each day.

Bernadette shrugged. The front and sides of the refrigerator were now mostly covered. A set of magnets featuring vintage-looking fruit crate labels held up the newest pictures.

Bernadette's mind flitted for a second on the word "prayer," but she knew better than to say that to her brother, even in her current state. She repeated silently to herself, *Wake up. Wake up. Wake up.*

"This is creepy, Bern." He opened the door and poured her a glass of orange juice. "I'll stay and watch TV until I'm sure you're all right. You hungry?"

She shook her head, and her brother disappeared to the living room. Bernadette could see that something about her new hobby was unusual, but the faces formed a comfort. She wanted to defend herself, but saw no real need. She flipped through her purse. She found the pamphlets she'd pulled from the rack at the doctor's office, close-ups highlighting the unlined smile of an older woman, the plumped cheeks of another, the before and after of a man with a restored hairline. She would wait until her brother was gone, and fit them into the fold.

Bernadette decided to take a nap. She informed her

brother of this decision, and he let out a sigh of inconvenience. A nap might take a while, but he didn't fight her.

Bernadette crawled into bed with all her clothes on: a nice button-up shirt she wouldn't have to lift over her head if her face had been tender and drawstring linen slacks that were comfortable, ironed to crispness that morning. She loved how linen looked so clean when freshly pressed, but hated how quickly it degraded into wrinkly sloppiness. All the same, she wore it often. She thought linen lent her the air of a woman more sophisticated than she actually was.

In a dream, Bernadette revisited the well-coiffed man from the waiting room. He told her how much he admired her for her natural beauty, that he was tired of all the women who looked the same, as if an assembly line had spit them out but was getting a bit out of sync, so that from one to the next, the eyes were just a little out of place, or the pink of the lips was printed just a hair to the right, making it obvious that *something* was wrong, but difficult to detect *what*. Bernadette, though, he said, was obvious, her minor flaws easier to look at, real. And then the man turned into a donkey, and then Bernadette got lost in a jewelry show where Oprah was interviewing an old friend from high school, and then she woke up. Bernadette ignored the events that ended her dream, but drowsed in bed thinking of that man wanting her, deciding he saw something in her that matched his desire. She emerged from her bedroom to find her brother already gone.

She returned to the kitchen and ripped carefully around

the fold lines of the pamphlets. She fit them in white spaces between existing pictures on the fridge. She sat at the table and regarded her handiwork. She felt an ache, an identifiable want, and approached the refrigerator again. She removed the original drawing she'd made of the handsome man, and fit it perfectly in her palm. She reached this hand beneath the waistband of her rumpled linen pants, and she allowed the man to show her his affection, while everyone else watched.

GLADNESS OR JOY

A YOUNG MAN AND WOMAN SIT AT A BAR, A setup for a punch line.

They trade names of books they've enjoyed recently until they find one on which they can agree. "I've never read a domestic story that's happy, though," the man tells the woman.

"I've never read any story that's happy," the woman says, and they laugh. The young woman searches in the young man's statement for what she believes might be an accusation—that women should be happy to have the privilege of keeping a home—but she cannot find such an insinuation embedded in his words or demeanor, and so they finish their drinks and order another round.

They date for a respectable amount of time and then marry. They have a child. Their child starts walking, and the first time he takes a spill, the husband's eyes tear up, though the child is unfazed.

Is my husband too kind? the woman thinks, but she has come to recognize this habit in herself and slaps her own hand.

✦

BY THE TIME the family arrives home from the store, the frog is dead. *Why would I think it was a good idea to buy an animal at Walmart?* the mother asks herself. Her child is bereft. He had already named the frog Puddincup. They don't even unpack the groceries, just reverse their course, returning to the store. They approach the customer service desk with the plastic-lidded cup, now reminding the mother of the wet specimen jars at the science museum, filled with two-headed cat fetuses and see-through fish.

"We purchased this frog less than an hour ago and it's dead. Can we have a refund?" She smiles apologetically at the child, but in her mind she is balancing her dramatic tendencies (*What is a life worth?*) and her pragmatism (*How attached could my child have become to the pet in less than an hour?*).

The child places the cup on the counter. The bored employee nods like nothing is out of the ordinary and asks if they have their receipt.

Disgusted by the request, but also realizing the receipt is in one of the grocery bags in the car, the mother clucks, "Never mind," and ushers her child back out to the parking lot.

✦

A WOMAN HAS grown blind to the advertisements and sweepstakes that ghost around the margins of her browser until one day her vision acknowledges them again and she asks a coworker, "Does anyone ever win these things?"

A moment passes before her coworker responds. This is the speed of their workday: the chitchat nearly constant, but irregularly paced as one or the other of them finishes writing or reading an email. When they're entering data they can keep the conversation moving at a quick clip, the task requiring only visual cortex and muscle memory. "No, no one wins those contests. They just want your information."

The woman nods and then quickly fills out the entry form for a trip to Rio. *I can always unsubscribe,* she thinks.

Months later she receives an email that tells her she's won. The message addresses her personally, features a typo, and is signed by the assistant to the head of marketing at the Brazil Board of Tourism. She calls her coworker over. "Does this seem legit?" She remembers the time she scratched off a lotto ticket, sure she'd won a cruise, only to find the fine print informing her that what she'd won was an entry into a secondary lotto drawing to win a cruise. She'd thrown the ticket away.

Her friend has to read the email three times to understand. "You won a trip to Brazil?"

The woman balks. "Probably not. I'll email them back, but it's a hoax, I'm sure."

It takes about a week for the details to come together, but all of the communications indicate that, yes, the woman has won a contest held by Visit Brazil. For ten days she will be put up in a hotel of her choice, an all-expenses-paid trip for only one attendee. Though she implores her friends to come along, none are able to scrounge up the cash quickly enough. The woman prepares to go alone.

"You're going to end up coated in rainbow feathers and locked in a birdcage," jokes her coworker. "Nice knowin' ya!"

The woman laughs. On the plane she tells herself that if she dies on this trip, then it is meant to be. There are fates worse than death, but rather than finding comfort in this self-supplied sentiment, she spends the rest of the flight imagining possible fates that would be worse than death.

A guide from the Board of Tourism, a young man named João, accompanies the woman for the entire week, excited to show her both the major attractions and the hidden treasures of the city. He invites her out with his friends one night, and, drunk on caipirinhas, she declares this evening one of the best nights of her life.

A canceled flight delays her return home and she misses an extra day of work, but her boss says it's no big deal. "How did you break out of your birdcage?" her coworker jokes.

"Turns out it wasn't locked!" the woman says, and remembers the worry she'd toted all the way to South America.

✈

A COUPLE WATCH a movie together. In the beginning of the film, a dad warns his son against texting and driving. Later in the movie the son looks down to type a message while piloting a car down a country road. The couple watching clasp each other's hands, bracing themselves for calamity.

But nothing happens. The text is sent. The kid arrives safely to where he's going. Everything is fine. The movie ends. "I liked it!" the woman says. The man agrees.

✈

A WRITER GOES on tour to support a new collection of short stories. Back in a small bookshop in a comfortable neighborhood of his own city, he takes questions from the audience, three-quarters of whom are friends of his, the remaining portion comprised of people he assumes took a seat out of curiosity and now feel obligated to stay. A coworker accuses him of writing only about tragic events, even if his treatment is often comic. "No one is ever happy in your sto-ries," she says. "Are you okay?" The audience recognizes their cue to laugh and the author takes the question in stride.

He regrets citing *Anna Karenina* and its theory about happy families, but does all the same. He talks about the need for conflict to drive narrative. "Has anyone read a novel about only happy people?" he asks.

A woman the writer didn't even think was listening, splayed across a stuffed chair in the corner thumbing through children's books, speaks up. "Sure. *The Joy Experiment*!"

The author smiles warmly. "That's nonfiction, though, right?"

The woman responds, "Yes, that's right! One of the best books I've ever read." Her face remains sunny and expectant. The writer glances out at the rest of the audi-ence, and freezes his expression, trying not to show his resistance. He has no interest in embarrassing or arguing with this woman. He sees a pair of people turn to each other and snicker. An old college acquaintance, so sweet to come all the way from the suburbs, catches his eye and raises his brow, eager to see how the situation will be han-dled. The writer thanks the woman and says he'll have to check it out. She gives a quick nod, satisfied at the success of her counterargument, and continues reading the pic-ture book in her lap. The writer asks if there are any other questions. There are not.

YOU HEAR YOUR name shouted from across the street. The doorbell rings. The deadline passes. You taste the soup for seasoning and somehow you got it right on the first try. "Listen to this," your friend says. You wait.

DEFAULT

EVERY MEMORY TWISTED BY REVISION. SAYING GRACE in the drive-thru. Bright sleep with the TV screen shining an ice rink. The way his language always blurred away from promise. A pink cassette player I tried to keep, but he insisted I give to my sister. Honor roll notices from the newspaper mailed to me, like he could teach me my own life, too. Random news articles tucked in—always something I knew about, but a week later, after it had already changed. Batteries not included. No cash for my textbooks, but an invitation to watch the pay-per-view fight on Saturday night. Grass stains dragged down my ass. Relief flickering through disappointment when I heard his car's engine failing to apologize. Free buttons he picked up at trade shows wrapped in tissue and string. Suburban curry buffet and Goodwill Supermarket Sweep. Voice-mail box full. Ghosts halved and halved and halved again. Dirty geometry. Static tragedy. Splinters polished to a flash. Made in China. Scratching tickets and unshrinking ground beef gray with age. Sister logrolling down the hill. Mom in real life. Fairy tales about him. Nosy neighbors asking if he was back. Hundred-and-ninety-proof. Polyester. Spoilsport. Peeling his nails on the couch and flicking them at the screen, at me when I complained. Mom vacuuming. Stale donuts and an outdated globe. Give it a spin. Close your eyes. Plant a finger. Rhodesia. Too bad. Front yard. Red light. Green light. Loans in Monopoly. Only college football on Saturdays. Baptism money emptied from my savings account. Spinning quarters at chain restaurants. Picking coins out of peanut shells on the floor. Trivia at Cliff's Tap and a beer for me because he knew better than the law. Unsealed packaging. Laundromats and still-damp sweatpants. Sister eating Kleenex. School counselors. Saturday stomach cramps like clockwork. I don't owe you anything. Flammable. Sister drinking a vanilla shake and a cup of water for me. Even the scrambled eggs burnt, the instant ramen watered down. Glued to the back of my seat with acceleration. Tight corners. Loose timelines. Opinions on strep throat. Breast is best. Pretending I understand soccer rules. Anything not to talk. Learning soccer rules. Dead batteries. Snowy April. Illegible goodbyes on the backs of receipts.

I made all these notes and decided no one deserved them, even me. A priest he'd never met gave the eulogy: a Mad Lib of lies with his details filled in.

In the car on the way to lunch afterward, my sister turned to me with tears in her eyes. I couldn't believe she was as sad as she seemed.

I said, "He was awful to us. Me especially, but you, too. It's good we're finally done."

My mother drove. We thought it big of her to attend at all. His girlfriend had made the arrangements. Everything red satin and roses. She had a ring on her finger that we knew would disappoint her at the pawnshop. She said our flowers hadn't been delivered, and we pretended we'd ordered any.

Who were all those people? How had they found out? He claimed not to have a cell phone. Didn't seem like an address book was likely. Maybe slips of paper taped on the inside of a cabinet door, fluttering like feathers each time he pulled out a mug.

"It's not that," my sister said.

I saw my mother blaze in the rearview mirror.

My sister's tears bulged fatter. She trapped her face in the back of the seat in front of her. "He wasn't your dad. Not really," she said.

I didn't even register shock. It felt so immediately true: I'd never wondered, but suddenly it became clear that such a question had been one more responsibility bestowed on me unannounced, one more way I'd failed.

I found only a single chip of disbelief in this otherwise flawless news. "How did he keep a secret like that?"

My mother said nothing, her eyes screaming straight ahead.

My sister sheltered my hands with her own. "He didn't know, either."

A sorry inheritance.

MAULAWIYAH

THE RESIDENTS WEREN'T *REQUIRED* TO TURN IN their electronic devices, Ron said. The retreat was not going to enforce any of its suggested guidelines. However, if participants thought they might have trouble committing to a break from technology, they were encouraged to drop laptops and phones and tablets off here or later in the office. The retreat would work better if residents disconnected.

Raila wanted someone to *force* her to be disciplined. She watched as the other residents filed up to turn in their technology. She looked at the phone in her lap to see missed calls from her dad and Jacob, and slipped it back into her pocket.

This policy was relayed in the welcome session before dinner in which Ron laid out other basic guidelines: Participants were urged not to knock on each other's doors. If they felt like going for a walk, he recommended they find companions in the main lobby. Knocking on someone else's door meant you were prioritizing your own schedule over someone else's. You might disturb your fellow residents' practice.

Raila turned to Lisa to whisper, "What exactly do they mean by *practice*?"

Lisa mouthed the words *Alone time*, with a lift of her eyebrows and a short exhale. Raila made a note of this simple translation, but found herself winding around her own confusion as to whether they meant practice as in "repeated performance for the purpose of acquiring proficiency," like the way a child practices the piano each night, or "the exercise of a profession," like a doctor's business. Was she supposed to be learning a skill or demonstrating her mastery of it? Already she felt unqualified.

The session wrapped up and Raila blinked out of her preoccupation.

"That's a lot of rules for a relaxcation," Lisa said.

Raila had signed up for this wellness retreat as a way to disconnect from her father. She hated how insensitive she seemed, but three months later, her father still insisted on repeating the same litany of things he would have done differently if he'd known Raila's mother wouldn't be alive when he woke up that next morning. Raila understood that people mourned differently, but she was exhausted and found herself more affected by her father's grief than by her own loss.

The moment Raila walked in the door of the lodge, Lisa, petite, wiry, and wild-haired, had introduced herself. "Finally!" Lisa had said. "I've been drifting back and forth from the kitchen to my room, wondering when another resident would arrive! Isn't this spectacular? Can you believe the light?" Raila raised her eyes to the thatch lining the rafters. Pale adobe tile stretched out onto a veranda. A stiff, warm breeze paced through the lobby. "You check in over here," Lisa had said, leading her to the front desk. While Raila tried to relay identifying details to the clerk, Lisa bent to pet a golden retriever beside the desk. "This is Sam-oo-ell! Isn't he handsome?" The clerk handed Raila her key and Lisa interrupted to say she knew just where the room was.

"Enjoy!" said the staff member, whose name tag read *Ron*. Lisa led Raila all the way down the hall to the right of the lobby.

"Well, shoot, these rooms end at fourteen. Your room must be on the other side." They trekked back, and Raila glanced at Ron behind the desk, smiling at them, oblivious.

"Thanks!" Raila said when they arrived at her room. She let herself in and lifted her suitcase to the bed.

Lisa still lingered in the door. "Your view is much better

than mine. I can only see the cars pulling up in front of the lagoon."

Raila shrugged. She knew she'd paid the higher price for an ocean view. She commenced unpacking her bag, careful to leave an emergency package of Oreos covered by a sweater.

Lisa revealed herself to be the same age as Raila. Raila was always a bit surprised when someone bothered to ask the question, not because she cared about others knowing how old she was, but because she couldn't see what difference it made. Lisa clutched her mug of tea with both hands and chattered away. "I'm here this week, but then I'll only be home for a week before my family takes a vacation to California for two weeks. If you have any ideas of what would be fun to do in California, I'm all ears. I haven't put any planning or research into the trip yet. My *husband* bought the four of us tickets to L.A. He booked the trip on a whim—as an apology—despite the fact that we do *not* have the money."

I'd be pissed if my husband bought four cross-country plane tickets without talking to me first, Raila thought. "An apology for what?" she asked.

"He's been cheating on me for the past year, but—get this—with a woman from Southern California! Why would he want to take me to that place? It's going to be excruciating. How am I supposed to not think about how severely he fucked up, the entire time I'm there?" She let out a throttled scream. "I'm so *angry*. Being here, it's the first time

I've had a chance to breathe in months. I've really been trying to hold it together for my son and daughter. My son is ten. He's old enough to understand, but the arguments upset my daughter. So I try not to lose my temper, but that doesn't seem right, either. He should know how angry I am."

Raila decided it wasn't her place to offer up her criticism. Instead she said, "I'm so sorry. That's awful. I can't imagine."

Lisa threw up her hands. "Neither could I before it happened. A newborn daughter, and he takes up with a blond Californian, drinking rosé out of a plastic cup on Venice Beach. So wretched. He positively drained our savings with the trips. He said it was for business and he'd be reimbursed." She paused. "I'm going on and on. You unload on me now."

"Oh, ha. I'm here trying to refocus, get healthy, create some good new habits, tune the world out, reprioritize." Raila saw her chance. "I'm so sorry, but do you know where the bathrooms are?"

Lisa led her down the hall. Raila got the sense Lisa might wait for her, so, before she closed the door, she said, "See you at the info session!" She waited until she heard Lisa's footsteps retreat to release a warm rush of urine.

At dinner, the two dozen residents joked about how they wouldn't be able to make it a week without sweets. "I could already go for some chocolate cake," said a woman wearing a megawatt-green brooch tacked to her Dri-FIT top.

Raila thought, *She must have pinned it through her sports bra, too. There's no other way it could stay in place.*

Lisa broke in. "Fine! I will make us a chocolate cake." Everyone told her there was no need; it had been a joke. Aside from an opportunity to detox, this week was about protecting time for yourself, not sacrificing it to others. "No, no," Lisa had said. "You want a cake, I'll make one. If no one else will do it, I will. We'll have it for dessert tomorrow after dinner!"

Raila scanned the crowd of women indifferent to Lisa's insistence. Raila imagined the martyred way Lisa might tell this story to her husband. *Everyone wanted cake, but no one would make one, so of course, you know me, I had to,* she'd say.

Raila thought, *I won't eat that cake.* And then she realized, *There will never be a cake.* She felt better.

That night, Raila tried to fall asleep with her balcony door open, but at the first chirp of an insect, she pulled the glass shut.

Before Raila met the other residents for Sunrise Yoga on the pool deck, she put on a coat of foundation and some mascara, and then hated herself for doing it, but she reasoned the foundation had built-in sunscreen. Who knew how bright that Mexican sunrise could be? Her skin looked too even with the foundation, though, so she dabbed on some blush, too. The first lip product she picked up happened to be lipstick, so why go searching for the plain lip balm in the bottom of her makeup bag? Raila's even blond bob didn't need much tending to. She surveyed her arms and the way they'd begun to show shape. She didn't let her eyes stray below her waist, where she knew she'd be frustrated by what she found. Strength. She was doing yoga for strength, not to lose weight or look "better."

Raila kept up with the flow for the most part, though she chaturangaed from her knees rather than full plank. She'd picked up yoga when her mother had died, as a way of trying to let herself inhabit whatever she was feeling instead of avoiding it. She found it difficult to track such slow progress.

In ustrasana, despite the instructor's insistence that none of them were going to faint from the surge of adrenaline tweaked out of their spines, Raila bent forward into the comfort of balasana to rest. At the end of class, the guide walked around placing warm washcloths scented with lavender on their eyes, and Raila thought, *I will never leave this place.*

In an even, calming voice, the guide repeated, "Empty your mind. Let yourself think of nothing at all."

Raila circled her thoughts around the words, *Don't think, don't think, don't think,* and wondered if that was the same as emptying her mind. She certainly wasn't able to worry about anything other than her attempt to focus on nothing. Perhaps this was what realization of this goal looked like in practice. Maybe *thinking about nothing* actually meant *thinking about thinking about nothing.*

. . .

At breakfast, Raila piled berries and oats and honey into her yogurt. The woman next to her exclaimed, "Sorry! I'm hogging the hemp!" Raila took the box from the woman and sprinkled some seeds on her own bowl, uncertain of their purpose. Raila eyed the coffeepot, but helped herself to the leftovers of someone's apple ginger kale juice instead. She felt the sting of the ginger deep in her sinuses. When someone saw the tears in her eyes she lied and said her allergies had been acting up and the whole table sighed in sympathy.

After breakfast Raila retired to her room with the intention of reading the meditation book she'd brought along, but instead she flipped open her laptop, slipped in earbuds, and started an episode of the reality TV show she'd fallen behind on. A knock barreled through the door, bouncing off the high ceilings. Raila slid the computer under her bed before answering. There stood Lisa, her face still creased with sleep. "Fancy some yoga?"

"I did the morning yoga session," Raila apologized.

"No matter," Lisa said, like the danger was that Lisa might refuse Raila's company and not the other way around. "Yoga can be enjoyed more than once a day!"

On the deck, Lisa kept calling out the names of poses Raila had to crank her neck to follow. "You don't know this one, either?" Lisa said, pulling her head down with one hand and hanging her other arm at the crook of the first elbow. "Sleeping duck. It's a rest pose," she said.

Raila worked on her bakasana instead, balancing on her hands, and pulling first one leg to her elbow and then the other.

"Well, well," Lisa said. "Look at Miss Fancypants!"

Raila had only been able to get her feet off the ground for about a week. She'd been working on it, every day, during a full session of yoga and then again while watching TV at night, until Jacob spanked her butt and told her to relax. "This is relaxing!" she'd insisted. After all that work, she didn't love the feeling of Lisa making her out to be a show-off, so she stopped, took a sip of water, and started to roll up her mat.

"You can't quit. We didn't do corpse pose yet!" Lisa said.

Raila wanted to reiterate that she'd already done yoga that morning. She wanted to say that she'd like to fit a shower in before lunch and their afternoon hike. She could smell herself and didn't want to think about her body while they were moving through the forest, but Raila lay down on her mat and closed her eyes, and thought, *I smell, I smell, I smell*, and realized that that mantra worked just as well as *Don't think, don't think, don't think*.

At lunch, Raila struggled to get the shell off a hard-boiled egg to eat with her salad. Lisa passed her and said, "Next time, save me a seat!" Raila thought it was a rude thing to say, as if none of the other two dozen women in the room were worthy of Lisa's company.

. . .

Before they left on the hike that afternoon, Lisa asked if she could put her water in Raila's bag. Raila wanted to suggest Lisa go inside and grab a pack for herself, but she took Lisa's bottle all the same. When the path narrowed, Raila allowed herself to fall behind Lisa in line. Lisa kept turning sideways to gesture, but Raila felt distracted by worry, envisioning Lisa tripping on a root ahead of her. When Lisa said, "Do you get it? My *aura* is *neon*," Raila nodded, guessing at the right response. "You're supposed to *laugh*!" Lisa chastised her. Lisa retold the joke, and Raila mustered a chuckle, even though, still, she had not listened closely enough to understand, having been distracted again, this time by the mental rut of scolding herself for not listening the first time. "I'm a robot!" Lisa exclaimed, and a genuine laugh cracked from Raila. Lisa looked pleased.

That day's hike was a warm-up, to get people used to moving through the jungle terrain. Even so, they traveled six miles over the course of three hours, half of it uphill. Raila tired from carrying only her own body. After they finished their ascent, they emerged from the tree cover to find a matronly woman standing under the umbrella of an ice-cream cart. Raila wondered how the woman had made it all the way up there with a hand-pushed freezer.

Lisa busted through to the front and asked for a Choco Taco without hesitation. The rest of the group looked to Ron to ask if this was okay. Ron smiled. "You're the boss of you," he said.

The vendor shook her head at the mention of a Choco Taco, and Lisa said, "No Choco Taco in Mexico? That seems wrong. I'll take one of those, then." She pointed at a coconut paleta de crema instead, and had the wrapper pulled off before the paletera asked for the payment of twenty pesos. "Shit!" Lisa exclaimed, and looked back to the group. "Raila, do you have cash?"

Raila dug into her backpack and paid for Lisa's ice cream. An impulse toward proving her own austerity formed in the moment she forked over the two coins, and for once she shook her head when the ice-cream lady said, "Y tu?"

"Fine! Make me eat alone!" Lisa laughed.

Back in her room that afternoon, Raila checked her phone to find no missed calls. She selected her dad from the list of contacts and hovered her thumb over the CALL button, but then tucked the phone back into the nightstand.

At dinner, Lisa apologized to the woman staying in the room next to her. "I'm sorry if you heard my phone ring. It was because I had my phone on and it rang." The woman didn't tell Lisa it was fine. She didn't ask her to keep the phone on silent. She turned back to her food like she didn't care at all.

Lisa said to Raila instead, "It was my husband. He was calling to say he loved me, but I just can't reconcile the fact that he cheated on me but he still loves me." Lisa said all of this like it was brand-new information. "What was he *thinking*?" Lisa asked. "And she was so *plain*. I can't imagine what attracted him to her, but he would have gotten tired of her at some point. She just kept flirting and flirting, trying to convince him he wanted her. But she was so *plain*."

Raila balked at this line of reasoning. "Well, it's not about what she looks like, right? I mean, would it be better if she were devastatingly beautiful?"

Lisa flared. "I think it might be! Then maybe I'd understand."

"Do you have a picture?" Raila asked.

"Do I have a picture? Are you nuts? No, I don't have a picture of my husband's mistress!"

Raila saw through Lisa's vehement denial immediately. She knew that Lisa had screen-capped the woman's profile at the very least. Raila wanted to see a photo for the same reason she flipped through the mug shots in the local newspaper online each Monday morning. She liked to *see*, but she couldn't define what information exactly the seeing provided her.

"And he went *back to her* to break it off, *in person*, and he didn't tell me. Why wouldn't he tell me?"

Raila thought about all the things Lisa's husband had done wrong, and she tried to decide if breaking it off with his mistress in person was one of them or not.

"I feel so betrayed. And now we have to go to California, and I don't *want* to go to California. But the kids know we're going to California, so I'm not going to be the one to take that away from them. Maybe we could drive somewhere *from* California." Raila watched Lisa tug her hair, braiding a small chunk with one hand, the strands swapping between Lisa's fingers and then easily loosening when Lisa let go.

"How did the cake come out?" an older woman asked Lisa.

Lisa didn't skip a beat. "What with the ice cream this afternoon I thought we could wait for the cake until tomorrow. Geez, sweet tooth much?"

Raila thought, *Abandon hope of cake, all ye who enter here.*

After yoga and breakfast the next morning, Raila took out her checkbook and opened her bank account online. Her friends made fun of her for keeping track on paper, but it eased her mind. The online numbers tallied to forty dollars more than her paper sum showed, and any reasonable person would have forgiven such a trifle and gone on with their day, but Raila spent close to an hour tracing the prior month's expenses, trying to determine the source of the difference. Finally, after plugging everything into a calculator, she saw that she had accidentally subtracted a twenty-dollar credit when she should have added it. Over and over again. The same mistake.

She turned on a podcast about scientific misconceptions to distract herself and lay back on the bed. "It's not that leprosy attacks the extremities first," the scientist said. "Leprosy attacks the nerve endings. It stops those afflicted from feeling sensations of both pain and pleasure, hot and cold, and it's our hands and feet that we use the most and that are the most prone to injury, and so—burns and pinches and cuts and blisters—if we don't stop them from happening when we feel the first jolt of pain, then slowly but surely those small injuries add up. They become infected and then those extremities are the first to rot."

Raila wondered if Lisa was allowing herself to feel too much or not enough.

"You cannot take care of what you cannot feel," the man on the radio said.

Raila thought she heard something outside her door, but when she opened it, she found the hallway empty.

In line for dinner, Raila talked with a young woman. "Oh, it's raining," the young woman said, nodding toward the downpour outside. Raila never understood people's need to call out the weather, but she picked up her silverware at the end of the line and pulled out a chair at an empty table so that she and the young woman might sit together. Lisa interrupted her before she took her seat, though, calling out, "Raila, over here!" Raila apologized to the woman and made up a lie about how Lisa wanted to talk to her about something. Raila could see the simultaneous indifference and exasperation in the woman's face at being left alone at the table.

"I have had a rough afternoon," Lisa said. Raila watched the door, willing another resident to enter and sit down with the woman she had abandoned. "I keep thinking about how I wish we hadn't had to get rid of the dog, but we *had to*. It was a rescue, and we couldn't put it through the experience of living in another broken home. The children were beside themselves, but it just wasn't fair to Roland."

"Roland was the dog?" Raila asked.

"Yes! A beautiful Shiba Inu," Lisa said with a sigh.

"You gave up your dog?" Raila asked, trying to call up sympathy rather than anger.

"Yes! We *had* to. Isn't that awful? I hate my husband. If he'd kept his dick in his pants, we'd still have Roland."

Raila filled her mouth with food again and again until her plate was empty. She excused herself.

The woman whom Raila had abandoned joined her to walk back to their rooms on the other side of the lobby. Raila mentioned how excited she was for their hike the next day, especially the beach, where they planned to break for a quick swim.

The woman pointed to the window. "Rain's stopped," she said.

The morning sun shined brightly in Raila's eyes as she laid her yoga mat down on the sand next to the woman-who-always-wore-the-green-brooch. On her threadbare T-shirt, the heavy brooch flopped around, thudding against the mat when the woman flowed through to urdhva mukha svanasana.

In the middle of class, while Raila concentrated very hard and tried her best to raise her arms to the sky in vrksasana, she noticed flicks of movement beside her. The woman-who-always-wore-the-green-brooch was gathering her things in a hurry. Raila hoped she was all right and sent her a silent *Namaste*. After the teacher told them to lower first their hands to their heart's center and then, slowly, with control, extend their foot to their mat, Raila shook out her ankle and found the spot beside her filled with Lisa.

Save me a spot next time, Lisa mouthed to Raila.

This was the first Raila had seen Lisa at a morning yoga session. When they began to center themselves to try vrksasana on the other side, Raila felt distracted and kept tapping her foot to the mat to regain her balance.

At breakfast, Lisa said, "It took me a long time to master tree pose. Don't worry about it."

Raila rejected the idea of mastery in yoga. *It's a practice*, she said silently, having now reconciled the word. Raila poured extra maple syrup into her oatmeal and Lisa waved a snap in front of her and cooed, "Treat yourself!"

That afternoon, Lisa asked Ron if she could bring along his golden retriever on the hike. "Sam-oo-ell looks bored!" Lisa said, trying to persuade him.

Ron agreed to it. "You can bring him along, but you'll need to take full responsibility. I must remain available to help hikers."

Lisa clapped and Ron went to retrieve Samuel's leash.

"You said you've spent quite a bit of time in California, right?" Lisa asked as Samuel pulled her down the trail.

Raila shrugged. She'd been driven down the coast twice

in her lifetime, once when she was thirteen on a family trip and once fresh out of college.

Lisa jerked forward for the hundredth time and said, "I'm too small! Can you take Sam-oo-ell's leash for a while?"

Raila complied.

"So, where else could we go if we fly into L.A.?"

Raila listed places for the sake of it. "Palm Springs, Joshua Tree, Big Sur, Las Vegas." She wasn't actually sure how close any of them were to L.A.

"Do you know cheap hotels in those places?" Lisa said, distracted.

Raila said, "Uh, I can ask friends if they have recommendations."

"Oh good! Yes, let me know," Lisa said. "You need to accept my friend request! Did you see the photo I posted of our last hike?"

"You mean the photo you showed me at dinner last night? I told you I liked it," Raila asked.

Lisa said, "Well, yes, but you need to *like* it on Facebook. Otherwise, it's like you didn't see it at all."

"I haven't been using Facebook," Raila lied.

"Bullshit!" Lisa said, laughing. Samuel was lagging behind, sniffing every tree. The group was getting farther and farther ahead. "Silly Sam-oo-ell! I guess we've learned our lesson, eh? We shouldn't offer to take him out again."

At the beach, Lisa ran into the water, but Raila didn't know what to do with the dog, so she waited for someone to come back so she could pass off custody.

Raila thought of the afternoon she and Jacob and her dad had returned home from the funeral, of the way Jacob had offered to get them something to drink. Her dad had remarked about how Jacob sounded like her mother, always worrying about others. "Yeah," Raila had said. "Except Mom would have yelled at us for not having had a water bottle at the funeral with us so we wouldn't get dehydrated from the crying." Her dad always failed to see the little cuts her mom made even in her kindnesses.

Lisa returned and told Raila she should have tied Samuel's leash to a palm tree. Raila didn't think the leash was long enough, but she passed it off and ran for the waves.

Moments later, Ron called out a five-minute warning to finish up and dry off. Raila hid herself beneath the surface.

When Raila spoke to Jacob later, he said, "It's funny to imagine you walking a dog."

"That's because I don't *like* dogs," Raila said.

Jacob laughed, and his voice turned serious. "I accidentally mentioned to your father that you said you were having a nice time. I'm sorry."

"Jacob!" Raila said. "He didn't think I could use my phone! Now he'll call!"

"I know, I know. I don't know what I was thinking. I should get a few points for talking to your dad, though, right?" he asked.

A knock on the door interrupted and Raila whispered, "I need to go! There's someone at my door!"

"Love you. Bye!" Jacob said, and Raila ended the call.

Standing in her doorway was Lisa. "Naughty, naughty," she said, sliding one stiff index finger against the other. "Do you want to do the Tibetan Rites?" she asked.

Raila inhaled. "Sure."

On the lawn, the two of them spun around in a circle twenty-one times. Raila tried to pick a point of focus so she could keep her balance, but by the last rotation she was grateful to sit down and center herself. She closed her eyes but her sight still dervished beneath her lids. Lisa seemed unfazed. "That one's my favorite," she said, and Raila tried to think of the proper Sanskrit name for the exercise, but it wouldn't come to her.

Lisa moved through the final rites at such a clip that Raila wondered if she was trying to show off. She thought about saying, *You're supposed to move more slowly, with control, to get the maximum benefit*, but Raila wanted the exercises to be over and done. She continued at her own pace, and, rather than finishing the twenty-one repetitions of each rite, she stopped whenever Lisa stopped.

They walked back to the lodge to get ready for dinner and when they pulled apart toward their rooms, Lisa said, "Save me a seat at dinner?"

Raila would do no such thing. She said, "Okay."

Raila sat beside the woman-who-always-wore-the-green-brooch. The woman apologized to Raila for running out of the yoga class. "I hope I didn't disturb you, but I threw up! The teachers always say it'll never happen, but I'm proof it does."

Raila couldn't take her eyes off the massive green stones. She saw herself reflected a million times, like in a fly's eye.

Lisa passed on her way to another table and sighed dramatically at Raila. When Raila went back to the buffet for seconds, the woman-who-always-wore-the-green-brooch followed. "Do you think Lisa finally made us that cake?" Raila whispered.

The woman-who-always-wore-the-green-brooch said, "Who cares?"

The woman in line ahead of them guffawed and turned back to them. "Karen voted against cake. Maybe her wish came true."

Raila said, "Who's Karen?"

The woman-who-always-wore-the-green-brooch said, "I'm Karen."

"Of course, of course. I don't know what I was thinking," Raila said, trying to recover, and she repeated to herself, *Karen, Karen, Karen.* She looked back to the table and saw Lisa hustle into the empty seat that held Karen's napkin.

On their return, Lisa grasped Karen's arm, and Karen nearly dropped her plate. "I'm so sorry," Lisa said. "I really need to talk to Raila. Would you mind?" Karen looked at Raila with a question and then she went to sit with the woman who had known her name.

Lisa whispered to Raila, "Do you know where we might stay for a few days outside of L.A.?"

"You already asked me that," Raila said, confused.

"Or, I was thinking we might stay with my best friend in Hollywood so we wouldn't spend more money. I think that might be the smartest idea."

Raila's mind exploded at the thought that Lisa had a friend in L.A. all this time that she could have been asking for advice. Outwardly, Raila smiled. "Yeah, that sounds nice and easy. You should go with that."

The sun set late there and a small group planned on hiking to a nearby plateau to watch the sky as the colors changed. Raila told herself she should go. When Lisa whispered, "I feel like watching a movie. Do you wanna do that instead?" she almost gave in, but declined.

Lisa nipped her napkin at Raila. "Suit yourself, overachiever."

In the morning, Karen eyed the empty spot next to Raila's yoga mat in the coveted back row, but Raila whispered, "I'm saving the spot."

Lisa didn't show up.

Lisa cut into the breakfast line to join Raila. "That was a good class, wasn't it?"

"I didn't see you—"

Lisa cut Raila off. "I think your balance is really improving."

Raila thanked her, unable to think of any other response. "I'd trade this quinoa porridge for some leftover cake, how about you?" Raila whirred with the high of asking Lisa about the cake.

Lisa piled strawberries into her bowl, like she hadn't heard. "Do you think these are grown in the U.S.? I'm really trying to be better about supporting local American farmers," Lisa said.

Raila cocked her head. "I would bet that those strawberries *are* local, but that would mean they were grown in *Mexico*."

"Agh, well, I guess we all just do our best and that's all that can be asked of us," Lisa said.

Raila decided to skip lunch that day. She was maxing out on small talk. *Small listening was more like it*, she joked to herself. Instead she ate a row of Oreos. She smiled, pleasant and closemouthed, at herself in the mirror—*mirror face* was what Jacob called it, claiming it was the only time she formed that expression, tilting the corners of her mouth up, squinting her eyes just enough not to form wrinkles, inhaling slightly to narrow her nose—and then she bared her teeth, the black cookie crumbs darkening the valleys between them, making her appear ghoulish and guilty. She set to vigorously brushing away the evidence. She checked her phone and wondered why her father hadn't called if he knew, thanks to Jacob's slip, that she had reception here.

. . .

On the hike that afternoon, Raila fell behind the group and reveled in the silence, admiring the braided shadows of the hanging vines dangling above them. Soon enough, Lisa joined her.

"Talked to the hubs today. He says he and the kids are doing fine, but I'm sure it's hard on him. He's never complained so little. I suppose it must have to do with his shame. I'm sure he's angry at himself, but I really can't make myself feel sorry for him, no matter how hard I try."

Raila reassured Lisa that her husband didn't deserve her pity and her belly let out a rumble, like an aluminum baseball bat clattering to the ground.

"What was that?" Lisa looked at Raila with horror.

"Oh, it was my stomach. Sorry. I didn't eat lunch and I think I'm crashing. You don't have anything with you, do you?" Raila asked, the sugar withdrawal jittering through her.

"I don't!" Lisa said.

Raila told herself she just needed to sit down until the feeling passed. She sipped her water and Lisa sat beside her, carrying on about her plans to go hiking in Griffith Park. "That's cheap, right? Provided we don't get attacked by a coyote?"

When the group was no longer in sight, Raila got nervous. "We should catch up. I don't know my way around."

"Don't worry about it." Lisa rubbed Raila's back. "I've got a great sense of direction."

"I think we can still catch them," Raila said. She stood

from the rock and pushed herself to a jog. When she reached Karen, straggling at the back of the group, she looked behind her and saw she was alone.

Karen noticed that Raila was out of breath, and said, "Tough hike today, huh?"

Raila agreed, and trudged alongside Karen, with her sensible walking poles and CamelBak.

At the top of their climb, their vantage gave a clear view of the valley below, but the path they'd hiked hid under the canopy of trees. Ron counted the group. "Twenty-eight," he said. "Who are we missing?"

People looked around, but none could come up with the name of the absent party, and so finally Raila said, "Lisa?"

"Ah yes! Of course," Ron said. "Well, we'll take a little break until she catches up. Enjoy. Have a snack. We'll be descending in no time."

Ten, fifteen, twenty minutes later, though, Lisa still had not appeared. "Now would be a moment when our cell phones might come in handy," Ron joked.

Raila knew Lisa probably had her phone in her pocket. Raila also had her phone in her pack, but she couldn't bring herself to admit it. Besides, she reasoned, they probably didn't have reception all the way up here anyway.

"Maybe Lisa turned around," Ron suggested. "I don't want to take any chances, though. I know we were supposed to stop at the underground river on our way back, but it would be best if we returned the way we came to keep an eye out for her. Sorry, everyone."

The hike back seemed totally new, approaching from the opposite direction, but Raila had booked the trip specifically to see the cenotes, and she cursed Lisa for causing the group to miss them. At the bottom of the hill, when they were back under tree cover, Raila tripped on a root and caught herself. She paused to rotate the sharp pain out of her ankle, and tried not to limp as they finished the last leg.

Raila's eyes adjusted to the interior light of the lobby. Lisa sat nestled into one of the big couches, reading a magazine.

"Lisa! Glad to see you're safe!" Ron said. "Did you enjoy the hike?"

"I did!" Lisa said simply.

Raila admired Lisa for a moment. Raila had a way of overexplaining everything so that even when she was telling the truth, she thought people suspected her of lying. Awe marbled Raila's frustration. She looked around, waiting for someone else to say something, but most of the others had scattered their attention.

Lisa smiled at her. "Feeling better?" she asked.

Lisa didn't mention her husband or the trip to California that night. Raila found her shoulders hunched, bracing for the topic to jab through, as it always seemed to. Instead, Lisa told a riveting story of her time working for a state senator, and his peculiar habits: the hours and company he kept, the way he treated the staff and admitted to wrongs privately that he denied publicly. "You know that saying, *The personal is political*? I wonder if politicians think they're exempt from that. It really seemed like he hid in the shade of his policy. He'd become deluded, thinking he did enough high-level good that he could get away with being a barbarian on the sly."

All evening Raila waited for Lisa to bring up her husband, but she never did, and when Raila returned to her room, she found she couldn't sleep.

She turned on the light and thought of calling her dad. It was nine o'clock here, so that meant it was ten o'clock at home, later than he usually stayed up, and she knew the trouble he had getting to sleep.

It was hard for Raila to understand her father's grief. Her mother had never been especially kind to either of them. She'd held fierce double standards, picking apart in others qualities that she herself possessed. When Raila had left for college, she'd loosened her bonds to her parents to such a slack that many of her friends felt compelled to comment on it. Raila phoned her mother and father every couple months, ignoring the voice mails from HOME that pocked her call history until she felt ready to connect again. "You've changed," her mother told her, and Raila thought, *If I've changed, it's that I'm willing to stand up to you now. I can see how you wouldn't like that.*

Whenever Raila's mother saw fit to evaluate her in some way—whether to tell her she'd grown cold and unsympathetic or to compliment Raila on some talent that had recently received outside recognition—rather than fighting back or thanking her mother, Raila had a habit of saying, "We're more alike than you realize." More than once her mother had hung up on her, as if the idea of them being similar—good or bad—were too awful to entertain.

On the last day of the retreat, the residents planned to do a group meditation after dinner, and then drink tea and talk about the intentions they were setting for their return home.

Raila wished it were the kind of place where they broke out a bottle of wine on the final night, but after morning yoga, she sat down to work on some resolutions, though it was hard for her to imagine following through on them. It felt like a performance.

A knock at her door startled her from her notebook, and Raila wondered what would happen if she didn't answer. She stayed very still. She wondered if Lisa might open the door to look inside, but she took that chance.

Footsteps retreated down the hallway and she tried to figure out how long she would need to stay sequestered to avoid suspicion. She skipped lunch again, popping into the kitchen just before the hike to pilfer some granola and a banana.

Out on the trail, Raila looked for Lisa, but didn't see her.

At dinner, when Lisa still hadn't turned up, she asked Karen if they should be worried.

"You didn't hear?" Karen said. "Her daughter was sick,

so she decided to head home early. I would have thought she'd tell you first," Karen said.

Raila noticed the green brooch was gone. "Where's your pin?"

A moment of surprise registered on Karen's face. "It must have fallen off."

Raila offered to help her look for it, but Karen shook her head. "It doesn't matter."

Raila went back to her room after dinner. When she finally talked herself into going to the group meditation, they'd already circled the fire, eyes closed. She tried to sit down quietly, but gasped when she planted her hand on a sharp pebble. She saw some eyes open and took the blame on herself, before transferring it back to the other residents. They were supposed to be focused so deeply that such a disturbance wouldn't matter. After just a few moments, the group leader broke the silence again with an *om*. A chorus of voices joined in and the group sleepily awoke to stretch and pour tea.

Raila was always hesitant to go first, not wanting it to seem like she thought what she had to say was anything special. Only after the initial influx of volunteers, Raila said, "I'll go." People turned their attention to her. "In general, I am easier on others than I am on myself. I accept and embrace others' faults, but harbor anger at myself for not *doing* more and *being* more. Heading back home, I intend to be gentler with myself and more loving. I plan to take the time and energy it requires to be truly good, making healthy meals and exercising and practicing mindfulness, rather than rewarding and medicating myself with quick fixes like alcohol and fast food and television. Thank you for your company. I wish you all the same permission."

The group said, "Thank you, Raila," in unison.

The young woman who always remarked on the weather started talking, and Raila looked at the empty spot beside her. She imagined Lisa there and scooted over to erase the thought. *Don't think, don't think, don't think.*

When the woman finished speaking, Raila sharpened her attention. The group thanked the woman, but Raila dropped off, realizing she didn't know the woman's name.

Raila's phone buzzed in her pocket.

HUNT AND CATCH

EMILY TAPPED THE KEYBOARD AT A STEADY RHYTHM. A page of meaningless strings of letters resulted from the three minutes that ended her day. She shut down her computer at exactly 5:00 p.m. She gathered her half-eaten salad from the fridge and tried not to make eye contact on her way out the door, avoiding the inevitable invitation to happy hour.

The back door of the office delivered her into the alley, a half block closer to her bus stop. When she glanced in the opposite direction, she spotted a dump truck. The man at the back of the truck pressed the lever to lower the lift and the dumpster landed with a clatter. He saw her, smiled, and waved, like he'd been expecting her, like they knew each other, like the moment he'd been waiting for had finally arrived.

Emily felt fear prick her skin, and she took off, walking swiftly in the opposite direction, afraid to look behind her. At the sidewalk, she made a right and wished hard that someone would join her at the stop, but the bus showed up quickly and she boarded, fumbling for her pass.

She spared herself the hassle of politely looking to the back of the bus for another open spot and allowed herself one of the accessible seats in the front.

A woman looked up and startled at the sight of her. "Aren't you supposed to be in jail?"

Emily furrowed her brow and shook her head.

The woman, still frowning, said, "Oh, okay. My bad."

An elderly couple beside her spoke quietly until the old man said, "Even blood has two colors," and the old woman agreed.

Emily lifted herself from her seat and moved backward as the bus skipped forward. She felt rubber drunk, boneless, movable.

When she looked out the window, the man in his garbage truck again paused, at the entrance to a different alley now. When he waved, Emily felt like someone had shoved the skin of her face in the direction of his hand. She felt the cartilage of her nose drag left and then pop back center. She let out a cry and looked around. The man across the aisle appeared to be locked deep inside his screen. Panic formed a mass in her chest and divided into her limbs. *I imagined it*, she told herself.

The man behind Emily answered his phone and his insistence distracted her. He kept saying, "Generally, I do both . . . Generally, I do *both* . . . Both . . . But *generally*, I do both." She waited for a clue as to what the man was referring to, but he clung to his abstraction.

When Emily got off the first bus, the tracker said the second bus wasn't due for twelve minutes. Emily ducked into the corner store and considered buying a bottle of water or a granola bar or one of the green bananas stacked near the register or a bag of pineapple-flavored beef jerky or a packet of almonds or a new charger for her phone to replace the one that dropped its connection and left her in constant fear of being stranded, powerless. She placed a bottle of lemonade and a bag of Skittles on the counter and asked the clerk for a bingo scratch-off ticket, her favorite because it took the longest to reveal whether she'd won or lost.

At the bus stop she drank half the lemonade in a single gulp, and remorse set in for the money ill-spent. She dug in her pocket for a penny, and came out with a dime and set to scratching off the ticket against the side of the bus shelter. She'd scratched off three of the sixteen bingo numbers when she heard a honk. The garbage man had parked his truck across the street and waved again. She felt her vision go black and her legs loosen beneath her. She reached for the wooden bench in the center of the shelter, and landed unevenly. She heard the squeal of the bus brakes approaching and she forced herself to stand and climb onto the bus with the center of her focus still prisoner to the darkness, only the perimeters fuzzily lit. She grabbed people's shoulders, blind. They shrugged her off and told her to watch it. The bus hadn't moved forward, and for a moment she worried the driver was waiting for the man in the truck to make his way across the street and board. She clutched a seat, waving her hand forward to make sure no one occupied it, and folded down, her head in her hands. She waited for her vision to supply information again, dim and skewed. She tried to see out the window, looking for the garbage truck, but she saw only an even row of sedans edging the curb. She pulled out her phone to text a friend and typed in the message, "I'm being followed. On the 66," but she didn't send it. She talked herself into believing she was overreacting. She didn't delete the words she'd entered, but she closed the messaging app and opened the tarot app instead. She pressed SHUFFLE three times and then chose her cards.

In the first position: Death. She knew better than to worry about this. The card heralded only a period of great change, but Emily was never sure what checking her cards so often meant for the time frame of their prediction. Did the deck know she looked at a new spread every day like a horoscope? Could it control itself enough to forecast only the following twenty-four hours?

In the second position: the Emperor. *Yes*, she thought, *I do want someone to confirm that I'm on the right path.*

In the third position: the Devil. She trusted the wrong people. She bought candy and lotto tickets instead of saving her money. She waited for it all to catch up with her.

The fourth position was supposed to show what was working for her, but she'd drawn the Tower, indicating disruptive change. She looked at the figures on the card being defenestrated, falling from the tall windows. That feeling of control dropping out rang true. Perhaps this was the way she operated best. Maybe she could embrace it.

In the fifth position: the Magician. Emily easily identified the man she believed was trying to trick her. Some cards were easier than others.

In the sixth position, she saw the Justice card and felt relief.

When Emily looked up at the LED sign, she realized she'd passed her street. She rang for the next stop and step-jumped down, not tall or strong enough to perform the movement with grace.

When the bus pulled away, she looked up to find the dump truck lingering in front of her. The man inside waved, and the night air swallowed her hearing. She fumbled for her phone and dialed 911. She changed direction, sticking with the main street, but the truck inched forward, close behind her. Emily tried to hear if someone was on the other end of the line, but the deafness stuck. She waited awhile and finally started talking without knowing if anyone had answered. "My name is Emily Baudot. I live at 5847 West Cortez. I'm being followed by a man in a garbage truck." She searched for a license plate or a truck number, but she found the vehicle unmarked.

About a block ahead, Emily saw a man walking his dog. She raced toward him and ended the call. She explained her situation, gesturing discreetly behind her, but the man seemed confused. She explained that she couldn't hear anything and asked if the man would walk her the rest of the way home. "It's only another block."

The man nodded and they turned the corner. At her gate, she thanked him and heard the dog whimper and a gust of wind quicken the leaves above her. "Oh, thank god," she said. She looked around and didn't find the truck. "Where did he go?" she asked.

"You can hear me?" he said.

Emily nodded.

"Honestly, I didn't see the truck you were talking about, but I wanted to help. I could come inside with you if you don't want to be alone."

Emily navigated swiftly to a new fear. She thought of the Magician card as her hand stamped the key into the gate's lock. "No, no. I'm fine. Thank you so much." She wedged herself through and the man grabbed the handle and held it open.

"Are you sure? I don't mind." He smiled.

Emily gave up on the gate and hurried for the vestibule. "No, thank you," she said. She unlocked the door and stepped inside. The man lingered at the foot of the stoop, his dog pulling at its leash.

"It's always better to be safe," he said.

Emily nodded and closed the door behind her, not stopping at her mailbox. She hurried up the stairs to her apartment and didn't turn the lights on once she'd locked the knob, the dead bolt, the chain. She made her way to the window. The sidewalk and street stood empty, no sign of the man with the dog or the garbage truck. She opened the refrigerator out of habit and remembered the candy in her bag and then the scratch-off. She retrieved both and ate the Skittles while scraping off the rest of the ticket by the light of the open refrigerator door, the cool air stealing the heat from her skin. The lotto card revealed a winning number, but the prize was only another ticket: an opportunity to repeat the poor decision she'd made.

She closed the refrigerator door. The quiet dark hovered close. Emily attended it.

UNDER/OVER

WHEN I FINALLY RETURNED TO MY STUDIO, THE piece I'd been working on had dehydrated and split at the edges. The dry, forced heat had triumphed over the tight plastic wrapping the clay. When I'd left it, I'd planned on returning early the next morning, but every morning since the accident, I'd lain in bed, beating myself up, until I went to wherever else I was required to be.

That day, two months later, I cleaned the studio from top to bottom. I hauled the feet of the figure I'd been working on into the trash. A teacher once told me that the mark of a good ceramicist is how much you're willing to throw away.

"It's not worth it to try to fix things that go wrong. Start over."

My brother said, "Switch places with me."

I was half asleep, drunk. "I can't drive," I said.

"You won't have to."

I noticed the flashing lights behind us reflecting in his pleading eyes.

"Brian," I said. "Shit."

"Please, Pen."

"What if they see us?"

"Hurry."

I ducked down and he bridged his body over mine as I slid onto the driver's side. I buckled the seat belt out of habit.

Brian had gotten a DUI the year before the accident. He failed the field tests and refused to blow in the Breathalyzer, landing himself an automatic "moderate risk." On the assessment tests he answered too honestly, admitting to drinking a beer or two most nights, up to eight in a single night on weekends, and was escalated two levels to a "high risk."

"I'm a bartender," he said, trying to reason with them, but the chart was the chart.

And so he had to go to seventy-five hours of therapy, rather than just the ten he would have been assigned if he'd lied and said he drank only on holidays. He was required to go to AA meetings, though he never stopped drinking.

When I made a joke about a program where all of the

attendees were just pretending not to drink because they were required to by law, he didn't laugh.

"I don't mind the stories. Some of these people have done wild stuff." He talked about smoking outside with pretty, clearheaded women. He talked about how men offered their phone numbers to call them when he was in trouble. He told me he avoided taking his turn at the meetings because he didn't want to lie, out of respect for the other members. I couldn't tell if this was because he thought he didn't have a problem, or because telling his truth would make it clear he did.

When the police asked if I'd been drinking, I said yes. I knew I stank of collated booze and Big Red. I was never a good liar. They asked how many, and I said three.

At my evaluation, I said five.

In therapy, I said someone else was filling my glass and I didn't remember.

All these answers were true in their own way.

We'd been on our way home from our mother's birthday party. Our uncle had developed a sudden passion for Fireball, and we kept cracking up at his insistence on refilling our glasses.

As I rolled down the window to talk to the cop, I had the thought that this was the biggest favor I'd ever do for someone.

. . .

We'd crashed into a concrete barrier. Our airbags had blown. The official report says I showed no remorse and little awareness of the severity of the offense. Me: the serial apologist, the girl who said "sorry" to a ref for committing a foot fault in high school volleyball.

In reality, I was stunned by my own willingness to cover for Brian. What the police officer registered was actually my resolve to do Brian this one, significant favor and my determination to make it seem as though the favor, not the accident, were no big deal.

In the police car, I didn't think about the discomfort of the zip tie around my hands or the hard plastic backseat.

Instead, I thought of Bernard Palissy famously burning all of his furniture so that he could fire his kilns.

Brian and I lived together. I puttered around, earnestly believing myself to be a working artist, not teaching enough ceramics classes to make ends meet, selling off designer clothes my mother had bought me when I was still in college to make rent. An occasional spot in a group show at galleries run by friends convinced my extended family I had promise. That uncle who'd poured the Fireball made the same comment every time I saw him, saying that he'd looked for my name on every placard at the Met, LACMA, the Art Institute, and I couldn't tell if he was serious or joking. My work was so different than the pots he expected to see a ceramicist making that he figured it must be real art, because he certainly didn't get it.

Brian bartended at a dive, the opposite of fancy. At home we subsisted mostly on frozen pizza, bags of lettuce edged in the pink threat of mold, and cream dressings, never bothering to wipe the congealed residue off the lip of the bottle. Sometimes I'd have beer and popcorn for dinner and he'd criticize me while making ramen.

I'd optimistically rented the two-bedroom by myself after undergrad, always nagged by the fear that I wouldn't be able to make rent the next month, too picky to take a chance on a roommate—friend or stranger. When Brian graduated with a political science degree we both knew he'd never use, I offered to let him join me. I *knew* I disliked living with him, but I knew that even if I told him that, our blood ties, at the very least, would remain intact.

Brian knew I hated when he referred to my work as a craft project rather than as art, and I knew he hated that I called him a mixologist when his bar so stubbornly served only well liquor and cheap beer. We established a cozy rhythm of insults.

The cop at the station turned to me unprompted to say, "You're not a bad person, you just made a bad decision."

My vision flared black for a second with rage at the accuracy of this platitude.

I asked for water and he told me I couldn't drink until my paperwork was finished. What he meant was he needed me to stay drunk until he had what he needed.

· · ·

I was required to get an evaluation, after the arrest but before the court date, to see how severe my drinking problem was, the same evaluation that had amped Brian up two levels from a moderate to high risk. I filled out the two-hundred-question Scantron, the last fifty questions measuring my cognitive ability. My cheeks burned with embarrassment at having to guess some of the vocabulary questions: abrogate, plangent, apodictic. Even some of the words I knew didn't match the synonyms the test offered.

While waiting for a counselor to see me, I furiously googled the words and eavesdropped as a man asked if beer would appear in his urine sample. Another asked to delay his drug test and the receptionist looked at him as though he'd lost his mind. A third kept talking to himself about how this situation was bullshit. "I just dropped that Xanny into the fifth of Rémy in my cupholder that one time. I don't even drink," he said.

"Oh yeah, that place is nuts," Brian said. "Who did your evaluation?"

"Ursula," I said.

"What'd she look like?"

"Older blond lady. She had lots of Polish chocolate wrappers taped to her corkboard."

"That's not who I had," Brian said, and turned back to the TV.

. . .

I had a show coming up. I was making large-scale human figures and I had to fire each section of their bodies individually. I emailed Kier some sketches. I was concerned they were too similar to the work of our mentor.

"Penny, Ramon doesn't hold a monopoly on the human form. His work is figurines. They're tiny, almost abstract. Your work has almost nothing in common." She was done with that topic and moved on. "Why haven't I seen you at the studio lately? You know you should block out kiln time for pieces this large. You'll have to candle those monsters for like half a day to make sure they don't explode."

Instead of being grateful for Kier's reassurance, I resented her behaving as though I didn't know how to fire my own work.

At intake, I took another test to measure my understanding of facts related to drinking and driving. To pass the program, I'd have to do better on the test at the end of the four weeks of classes. I got two of the fifty questions wrong on the test the first time and watched the counselor take out a calculator, shake her head twice at the number 96, and write down 98 percent. The straight-A student in me wanted that score, but I worried about improving. "I think I should have a ninety-six percent."

"Really?"

"Yeah, each question would be worth two points," I said.

"Oh, okay." She crossed off the old score and wrote down my suggestion, like it was a matter of opinion.

"What happens if I get the same score when I take the test again?"

She screwed up her face as though this were an impossibility. "You'll have to talk to someone," she said vaguely.

"Like go to more class?"

"I don't know. This is my first day."

I asked Brian if he'd accompany me while I completed the community service hours. "This is the part of the sentence that you could do with me. We could bond."

"That's stupid," he said. "Why should two of us suffer? Besides, I'm paying your fees, aren't I?"

"*My* fees?" I said. I felt the vacuous exasperation take over again.

"You know what I mean," he said.

All of the instructors who taught the Risk Education class and led group therapy were fresh out of a social work program.

In the STI class, Lela asked us what we knew about HIV. The class was silent for a painful amount of time and I knew if we waited much longer, the instructor would remind us that one of the conditions of the program was willing participation, so I said I didn't realize until recently that there was a drug that could prevent HIV, and the instructor told me there was no such drug.

"Yeah, it's called PrEP," I said, trying to sound agreeable.

"That just manages symptoms," she said. I could feel how happy she was to prove her authority.

When she left the room for a break, I showed the three other people who'd shown up that day my phone, proving that if you were at high risk you could take PrEP to prevent HIV, and they shrugged and turned back to their own phones.

Later that day, Lela listed the physical effects of alcoholism. I felt my face screw up with confusion when she said "psoriasis of the liver."

After a beat, I realized. "You mean cirrhosis?" I asked.

"Yes, psoriasis."

At home, I'd debrief with Brian in the early afternoons when he woke up. I'd tell him which class I'd attended the night before and he'd tell me about what he remembered from his time doing the same. "Did you watch that video with Martin Sheen? Did they show you the pictures?" Yes and yes.

Lela told us men held their liquor better than women, and when Bogdan, the Bulgarian man who chose a lion when asked what nonliving thing he would choose to be, said, in a husky voice, that he knew women who could drink him under the table, the instructor told him that was a myth.

"But what about tolerance? Or body size?" I asked. Other people around the table nodded.

"I guess that's true," the instructor relented. I was probably her worst nightmare: impossible to help, injuring her growing confidence as a teacher.

When she said her best friend also taught ceramics, I asked her name and she flushed, saying that she was professionally not allowed to say.

"Well, feel free to tell her I was in one of your classes," I said. "I bet we know each other."

"Gambling is also addictive," Lela said.

My mother found out about the accident from Brian, when he asked to borrow the money for the court fees. She asked to speak to me. "Be careful who you tell this to," she told me. "You have no idea how people will try to use it against you."

"Okay, to be clear, I didn't do anything," I said.

She said, "Well . . ." in such a drawn-out way I could tell she felt like my taking the fall for Brian was possibly an even worse error than the DUI. "I'll pay the fees. I didn't pay them for your brother, but I'll pay them for you."

"Again, not for me, but don't you think Brian should still have to pay?" I asked.

"Honey, he doesn't have that kind of money," she said, dismissing my suggestion. "But really: Remember that people will do anything to hurt you. They're only out for themselves."

"Okay, Mom. Thanks. I love you, too."

I hung up and wondered what could happen to me in my

life that would prompt me to feel that level of cynicism, that lack of faith in humanity. I knew it would happen. It was inevitable I'd become her. I wondered what would eventually force the transformation.

In every group therapy, in every class, every counselor was female. Otherwise, though, I was the only woman. Just me and a bunch of obligated guys in backward baseball caps and gym shorts. I drank my bottle of perfumed seltzer and they palmed cans of Mountain Dew.

I had done some volunteering before the accident, but I decided not to perform my community service at any of those places. I didn't want to have to ask people I knew to write letters confirming my time. I wanted them to know that I had been there strictly as a do-gooder. Instead, I looked for new opportunities. On the website for the local animal shelter, I saw that they recommended reading aloud to the older cats and dogs.

"You've got to be kidding me," Brian said.

"The website says it's legit," I said.

"And at your final court date when the judge asks you what you learned from your service hours?"

I didn't know the answer to this, but I also hadn't done the work yet. "What did you do for your hours?" I asked.

"Meals on Wheels," he said.

"They let you drive a vehicle around? That seems unwise," I said.

I showed up at the shelter the next morning and signed my name on the list of "Reading Buddies" under a bunch of eight-year-olds, but the woman working the desk didn't blink when I asked for my badge.

My friend sent me a link to the work of an artist with a show up in New York. "Thought you might like this," she wrote, and when I clicked the message, my heart stopped. This artist, too, made large-scale human figures.

I wrote back to my friend, "I need to rethink everything."

She texted right back, "Are you insane? I sent the link hoping you'd feel encouraged! This woman is blowing up!"

"Exactly. My work is derivative."

"OMG."

I took out my sketches and compared them to the pictures on my screen.

In the interview the woman talked about how her surfaces were busy, interrupted, refusing to rest, nothing smoothed down.

I'll make sculptures that are totally even and still, I thought. Sometimes simple opposites were enough to calm me.

After reading to the cats for ten hours, I realized I'd need to diversify my service time if I was ever going to finish it. At the Food Bank, the volunteer coordinator recognized me. "I saw your talk at the Art Center. I loved that show."

"Oh, wow," I said. "Thank you."

"So great that you volunteer, too!" the young woman said.

"Every little bit . . ." I said, and swallowed my pride. "I need to get a letter for court confirming the number of hours I volunteer here. Do you know how I go about doing that?"

The young woman's face fell. "Oh, uh, yeah. When it's your last day here, just ask for a printout."

"Thanks!" I said, averting my eyes.

Clusters of people wearing matching shirts laughed or sulked, employees participating in their companies' service days. We sorted and packed community donations: dented boxes of cake mix and cartons of fruit snacks missing a pack. The bank employees competed with one another to see who could pack the fastest, and I worried that they weren't checking the expiration dates.

It was just me and a big dude with a REDRUM tattoo who were there solo, and we came to the ambivalent consensus that zucchini bread mix belonged with sweets rather than with more traditional breads.

I went back most days for the following six weeks and recognized other regulars. There were retirees clearly just looking for something to do and high school kids working on a service project, but then there were others, in their twenties and thirties, there because they had to be. We never talked about why.

I volunteered to lift boxes of cabbage one day and learned my back couldn't handle three-hour shifts of weight-lifting produce. I sorted boxes of peaches so moldy they looked like they wore toupees, and squatted to dry-heave when others crumpled in my hands.

The other regulars and I learned which jobs took the least amount of effort. We ceded those easy positions only to the elderly. I liked breaking down the bulk totes of pasta and rice into two- to three-pound bags, learning the feel of an extra half ounce in the metal scoop, and nodding knowingly at the other regulars when someone new made a mistake.

When I came home from volunteering all day to find Brian on the couch, I'd share the highlights: Some old lady had asked why I was there and I'd lied and told her it was to get service hours for a work-related project. Our group broke the record for packing sweet potatoes.

"No offense, Pen, but these are possibly the most boring stories I've ever heard in my life."

I stared at him, but he didn't take his eyes off the TV, and so I gave up and looked at the TV, too.

I thought about changing my medium for the upcoming show. What if I painted instead? What if I sewed huge dolls? Stuck in my mind was the idea that a real artist didn't limit herself to only one format. A real artist challenged herself to move from clay to video to installation.

When I texted my friend this idea, she didn't respond

until the following day. "Unsubscribe" was all her message said.

I volunteered at a service fair that helped connect citizens returning from the prison population to the resources available to them. At a health-center table, every man I escorted grabbed the basket of condoms and mimed dumping them into his complimentary tote bag, posturing. The woman working behind the tables laughed politely, and I wondered how she mustered enthusiasm for the same joke over and over.

An older woman kept grasping my arm and asking if I was mad at her. "I know I failed that drug test. What will happen to me?" she asked. She filled her bag with flyers.

"I don't know," I said. "Maybe some counseling."

"I'm already in AA," she said.

"One day at a time." I felt useless to help.

Her head wobbled on her neck. "A day is too long, baby."

The gallery asked when I'd have photos of the work so they could start prepping promotional materials.

I complained to Brian that I had no time to get to the studio. "Just get the DUI stuff over with so you can get back to DIY." He grinned. "At least you don't have a normal job that you need to take days off from."

I sprinkled cilantro on everything we ate, knowing he would taste only soap.

. . .

In therapy, a painter showed no remorse for his drug and alcohol use. He loved the way they made him feel. He felt disconnected from his friends when he wasn't allowed to use, which was now, because he was being tested every week.

The rest of us sat in silence, not saying a word. It seemed like he was breaking the unspoken rule: Lie to save your ass.

A young guy with a chip on his shoulder and immaculately gelled hair spoke up. "This program is fucked because if we talk honestly about how much we drink or use, we risk being bumped up to a higher risk level and having to do more hours. But then if we're not honest, then the therapy isn't useful at all."

Even the counselor nodded.

In the spare hours of my day when I should have been at the studio making work, I watched TV. I had never been one to sit and watch television without some secondary task, some handwork or chore that needed doing, but in the hours after volunteering, class, therapy, I felt like a cymbal clang of my former self.

I bristled at the void of content coming out of the mouths of the people on-screen, and instead muted the TV and turned on public radio, trying to match up the sound track of talk show hosts with the sitcom, imagining them to be related: all a part of the same reality.

. . .

At group therapy, I implied that we were all there for the same reason, and the young man with the gelled hair said, "I'm not here for a DUI." He'd punched a door at a bar and a jealous ex had called the police. "She was just getting back at me for dumping her ass," he said.

"My mistake," I said.

"Well, I did get a DUI," he said, "but that was a while ago."

I judged him until my last day, when he told the group he'd set up sessions with a therapist to continue counseling after the mandatory period.

I didn't take any chances. If I were to get pulled over after having had even a single drink I knew I was doomed, so I abstained entirely.

I didn't tell anyone about what was happening. I considered lying and telling people that I had gotten a DUI, thinking it would be easier to explain than the idea of my taking the fall for my brother.

My friends wanted to know why I never had time to hang out and I claimed I was busy getting ready for my show.

My caseworker, Bonnie, was always convinced she'd catch me doing something wrong. I watched her actually say, "Doy," to her receptionist, bouncing her fist off her own head when the receptionist needed to be reminded of where to find a folder.

In our first meeting, Bonnie complained that she'd just

gotten a call from her brother asking what was for dinner. "He eats like a horse," she told me.

"My brother is the same," I said, hoping some early commiseration would serve me as our time together progressed. "And then he wants to split the bill, when he clearly ate way more than me."

"Oh, I pay for all my brother's food. He doesn't pay me rent. I even give him spending money."

"Oh, wow," I said. Empathy had failed me again.

Here was a woman who made a living telling people how to get their acts together. I wondered if she saw the irony in her inability to help her brother do the same.

She folded all my forms into an envelope and handed it to me. "Bring this everywhere with you: to class, to therapy, to service hours, and always—*always*—to visit me."

I'd already been keeping a folder of all the paper related to the case, and so I brought her envelope and my folder everywhere I went.

"The Victim Impact Panel is the worst part," my brother warned me. "Family members of people who died in drunk-driving accidents get up and cry and tell the story of what happened and how much they miss their daughter or their sister or whatever. It's rough. After that you'll never drink and drive again."

"I never have," I said.

"Right. Whatever."

"And you did drive again," I reminded him.

"Oh my *god*," Brian said.

I steeled myself. At the courthouse, the special events room filled slowly with close to a hundred people who had all driven drunk in the last month, everyone miserable, everyone warned about what we were about to hear.

And then: none of the family members showed up to tell us about their tragedy. The person running the panel was flummoxed. She tried to project a video of a recorded Victim Impact Statement from her laptop, but the sound wasn't working. We waited for close to a half hour for her to figure out the tech logistics, until finally we watched a video of a man explaining how he lost his whole family on the way home from Six Flags in a 1966 Volkswagen microbus. He kept repeating "1966 Volkswagen microbus" instead of saying his "car" or even his "van." I felt put off by his commitment to this detail and tried to remind myself that that wasn't what this event was about. A courthouse employee woke up the man beside me, warning him he'd be thrown out if he fell asleep one more time, but when he snored again a few minutes later, she just tapped his shoulder. When the video finished, they released us row by row from the front of the room back, like people exiting a funeral.

"Wasn't it awful?" Brian asked.

"Not in the ways I expected," I said.

· · ·

That night I drew a sketch of the man sleeping in his folding chair, imagining it one-and-a-half times human size in clay. I'd title it *A Man Sleeping Through What He Could Have Done.*

When I completed all the court's requirements in a record amount of time—the group therapy, the risk education, the Victim Impact Panel, the service hours—Bonnie hunted through my envelope looking for an error. "You need to pay your court fees," she said.

Brian had charged them to his credit card on the day of my sentencing. I hunted through my secondary file folder for the receipt.

"You don't need to bring that thing everywhere," she told me. "Only this envelope." She waved the packet she'd made near enough to my face that I felt a gentle breeze.

"But if I didn't bring this folder, I wouldn't have this." I pulled out the receipt for the court fees, and she snatched it from my hand.

She folded it into the envelope. "You shouldn't have taken it out of here."

"I didn't."

To this she had no response. I knew people must lie to her all the time. People were confused about what was required of them. All of the bureaucratic hoops were hard to make on the first jump.

"I know you're helping a lot of people," I said, and even *I* wasn't sure what I meant by that.

"Not a lot," she said. "Everyone."

When I finally returned to my studio, I couldn't imagine making art.

Instead, I tried to construct a gravity sink. This way I could fill a big watercooler bottle down the hall and save myself the many small trips each day.

I knew I should have been working on the pieces for the show, but by now the task felt insurmountable.

The first time I turned on the faucet, the water didn't flow, and I took the contraption apart and started from the beginning, unable to figure out what I'd done wrong.

My brother called to say he'd locked himself out of our apartment so he'd need to borrow my keys.

When he arrived at the studio, I had everything assembled again, but still water refused to flow.

"What am I doing wrong?" I asked him.

Brian walked over and took a quick glance. He squeezed the tubing between the bucket and the sink and water poured out.

I turned off the faucet and asked, "How did you do that?"

"There was air in the tube."

"How did you know?"

"Logic?" he said.

I thanked him and handed over my keys.

"I guess we're even," he said.

I'd never thought about what I'd done for him as something that would be repaid. In that moment I realized I didn't even believe in the idea of fairness.

"Even Steven," I said, and held out my hand.

"No problem," he said, and bumped my palm with his fist. He glanced around. "It's looking good in here."

My studio was completely empty of any work in progress. I hadn't even begun. He was admiring the tidiness of the space, but I knew a productive studio was always a mess.

KUDZU

"WE'RE THE INVASIVE SPECIES." THAT'S WHAT I tell my daughter while we hack through the vines into the light. For seventeen years we lived in a dark house, uninterrupted, the tendrils burying us deeper, until from outside I'm sure it appeared our home wasn't a home at all, but the simulacrum of a home, a topiary to remind passersby of a cottage, a fairy tale created by nature.

How long must something be kept from its natural habitat before it becomes foreign again? If the dodo bird were reintroduced within the balance of our current ecosystem, could it survive? Would it threaten other species?

Just after I pushed my daughter out into the world for the first time, I decided it would be best if we retreated. I would keep her safe from all of the outside harms. I found a cabin on a small bit of land in the forest. Already then, the kudzu had infected the area and so the property values had tumbled. I bought two goats, a sheep, some chickens, a rooster whom we'd need to learn to love. The goats would keep the vines at bay and the vines would keep the house well insulated and shaded: cool in the summer, warm in the winter.

We never used the word "weed."

I knew it couldn't last. I knew my daughter would eventually want out of this little world. I knew she'd go seeking the trouble I'd tried to keep her from, and I knew that was reasonable, but, in the meantime, we lived a happy life. We read. We built. We cultivated, harvested, and canned. We played and took long naps. We visited a ranger each week and passed her lists of what we needed, paying her for her time in baskets of vegetables and fresh eggs.

"But how do we pay for the supplies she gets us?" my daughter asked when she was ten. I could hold off the specter of money for only so long. It showed up in the books we read and I adhered to our honesty policy, so I could not pretend it was a fantasy, the way I had previously explained dragons and time travel.

"We are lucky," I told her. "Your grandparents were wealthy. If we live lean, mostly off of what we grow and create ourselves, then we will always be taken care of."

"Where are my grandparents now?" she asked, and we

continued her education on death, building on the idea of why it was important to be careful when walking in the woods, comparing their passing to the bird bodies we'd sometimes find on the forest floor, expanding on the idea of the chicks we waited to hatch and the eggs we ate before they'd have a chance. "And mosquitoes and flies and spiders?" She was putting it all together.

"Well, we try not to harm the spiders, right?" I asked, and she nodded solemnly, though reluctantly. She understood that the spiders would do most of the work controlling the flies and mosquitoes if we left them alone, but still, they bothered her. "The kudzu, too, is alive," I said.

"And it dies when the goats eat it?" she asked.

"That's right."

"But the goats do not eat us."

"No."

"And so we are stronger than the kudzu."

"The kudzu is even stronger than us, and that is why we honor it," I said.

The next day, I made it our project to dig up a full root crown of a kudzu vine, scooping the dirt away carefully to uncover its many arms. We traced its path far and wide, deeper and deeper, until my daughter looked up at me and said, "I understand. The kudzu goes on forever."

"Eternity powered by sunlight and chaos," I said.

Shrieking strains of cunning. Traces turned to choking. On days when I felt frustrated and afraid that even I could not keep my daughter safe, I feared the kudzu. I made metaphors and wondered if they applied to us or to the thick vines: outcasts on attack.

"Cultivating the land toward our own ends is another kind of conquest, our own sort of colonization and assault," I reminded her, and she asked again where we could go that was truly ours, somewhere that wouldn't be wrested from the control of another. I'd instilled in her that wherever we were, someone or something else had been there first.

On our walks, we'd occasionally run into a hiker. We never warned people off our land because we were never warned off other people's land. My daughter would wave and sometimes people would stop to talk. When she was young, she'd roam naked, and people would smile, assuming we were camping nearby.

"Is there a good swimming hole around here?" they'd ask, and we'd lead the way and then depart, letting them have their privacy.

"Can you point me to the closest road access?"

Sometimes we'd give directions, but sometimes we could tell the hiker desperately lacked skill, and so we'd walk them to the pavement, my daughter always shocked at the way the vines blazed along the edge of the road, stopping shy, maybe an experimental finger crawling out, only to be scared back by a semi or a mower or a spray of poison. If people didn't know what they were looking at they thought it was beautiful, but most experienced hikers saw the vines as a blight, an unfortunate effect they blamed on globalization, on our ineptitude at trying to share cultures.

"Not quite," my daughter would say, once she'd reached age thirteen.

"The Japanese brought it over," the hikers might say, sure they were helping my daughter learn.

"Well, kudzu *was* showcased at the Japanese Pavilion at the Centennial Exhibition in 1876, but it didn't become an issue until the 1930s when it was marketed to farmers as a way to slow soil erosion. It's no one's fault but our own. The government told farmers to plant kudzu, as much as they could afford."

The hikers would look at me for confirmation and I'd nod. Depending on their politics they might say something that led to a private conversation between me and my daughter later that afternoon on hate speech or on how even the best-intentioned people sometimes stopped short of looking for the truth.

The kudzu had a swagger we admired. When it crept in between the siding, we'd spend an afternoon clipping it back, letting the goats feast. We'd dry out thicker vines inside the cabin and save it for burning in the winter, save thinner vines to weave baskets we could take to the ranger. She'd fill her truck's bed and drop them off at the general store in town to be sold. We kept all the proceeds from those sales in a lockbox for my daughter's future. "But we don't need the money," she'd say.

"Someday you'll choose to live a different type of life," I told her, avoiding the true fear behind my words: that someday I might die, that I had only worked out how to stretch the money through my own old age. I knew that no teenager would choose to go on in this private way when there was a whole wide world out there. Even if she eventually returned, she'd set out to see what she was missing. I had gone to college and gotten little out of the experience, but she was bound to be curious, and I wasn't seeking to deny her exploration. To ease any guilt she might feel in leaving me, I tried to operate under the assumption that someday she would go.

On her seventeenth birthday, she started crying the minute she woke up.

"What's the matter?" I asked, pulling her into my lap like I had for all her life, both of us growing stronger day by day.

"I only have one more year with you," she said.

She had never confirmed before that she would leave, but her words didn't surprise me. I had all but talked her into it by that point, but it wasn't as though I didn't want her there with me. "Well, you can stay as long as you like. You know that."

"I thought you wanted me to go."

I cried, too. "No, baby, no. I want you to feel free. I don't want you hemmed in by my decisions. You can stay, but you'd also be fine out there in the world. You've learned what you can from me, but I can't deny there's more to know, and you can always come home."

She didn't talk for a day after that as her mind resituated.

. . .

I remembered taking the train when I was a kid, the way the bug-eyed Amish teens stared at my Walkman. I remembered how unassimilated they seemed and wondered if that was how my daughter would look to the outside world. Did we now communicate in ways that seemed strange and unapproachable?

I asked the ranger to get us bikes and we began to go into town, occasionally at first and then every day. We ordered tea in cafés and visited the library to use the computers. I was surprised how quickly my daughter picked up the skills she would need. A boy asked her on a date and she took down his phone number, with no way of calling it. We asked about a pay phone, but no one knew of one still in working condition. "Is it a local call? You can use our phone," the librarian said.

Back at home I asked my daughter if she thought she'd call him.

"I don't think so. I've been thinking I might like women." She seemed confident in her uncertainty and I was proud of her for knowing that this revelation would matter little to me.

"You could see if he'd be open to friendship, but a man's feelings are easily hurt, so it's up to you if you want to deal with however his ego reacts," I said. I thought it might be a good time for her to make a friend, and with a little effort he surely wouldn't be the only option.

At the coffee shop the next day she asked the barista if

she'd like to hang out sometime. The young woman seemed enthusiastic. "Definitely. Want to give me your number?"

I tried not to eavesdrop, but I found my ears leaning over. It was such a pleasure to hear my daughter talking to someone else, trying something out. It reminded me of when she was a baby, testing sounds and words to gauge my reaction.

"I don't really have one," my daughter said.

"So cool. I've been thinking about doing that, too," the barista said. "Um, want to plan on Friday, then? I get off around nine, so we could meet here?"

"Cool," my daughter said. "I'm Bug." It wasn't the name I'd given her. It was a name she'd apparently made for herself in that moment, and I felt the first pang of what it would be to live without her.

"Bug? Amazing. I'm Kate. I'll see you then if not before, I guess." Kate gave Bug a half wave and Bug mimicked the gesture with assuredness. I was amazed at how easily it all worked.

"I need a light for my bike if I'm going to ride at night," Bug said on our way out, and we stopped at the hardware store for a headlamp and some reflectors.

While she rode home next to me, I said, as nonchalantly as I could muster, "Bug, you know that you might attach to people pretty quickly because it's just been you and me."

"I was thinking about that," she said.

. . .

After her first meeting with Kate, Bug came home ener-
gized. She told me all the jokes they laughed at and I
smiled, though I had no idea what she was talking about.

I felt awe at the simple things that brought them both
joy: watching old cartoons Bug had never seen, flying kites
at night beneath the baseball diamond's floodlights, baking
together and then selling what they made to benefit the forest department. Instead of feeling like Bug was uncool or
out of the loop, Kate seemed to think Bug was next-level.
She thought Bug's interests were all inspired, rather than
childish.

Bug told me Kate had taken a year off after high school to
think about what she wanted to do. She volunteered at the
animal shelter and planned on studying veterinary science.
Kate was applying to schools, some of them far away.

"Does that make you think about what you want to do
next?" I asked.

Bug nodded. "It's hard not to think of just applying wherever she applies," she said.

"You should probably figure out what you want to study
first," I said. "I suspect one of the reasons I didn't love college was because I picked what I wanted to do and I picked
a school, but I didn't think about how one had anything to
do with the other."

"But you use what you studied all the time," she said.

I said, "Yes, but you can do other things while you figure out what you want to study in college."

"But I'm already so far behind," she said.

I'd never heard her express a feeling like this. It had crept in so quickly, like the vines after a storm. "It's not a race," I said. "Or if it is, it's a thousand races at once, and they all measure different things and you're ahead, baby. You're placing first in categories where other people haven't even stepped across the start line."

"I'm not sure what you're talking about," she said.

I laughed. She was a teenager after all.

Bug started working at the coffee shop and volunteering at the library. Kate went to the other coast for school. They wrote letters to each other. Bug thought she might like to become a librarian. "Well, you can study just about anything and become a librarian eventually," I said. She smiled big.

With the money she earned at the coffee shop, she booked a trip to visit Kate for a weekend, and then to travel the coast for a month after that. She bought herself a cell phone. She packed a bag and for the whole week before she left, she kept hugging me hard. "You're strangling me!" I joked, and she'd hug harder.

The ranger arrived to take her to the airport and I didn't watch them drive away.

I went inside and turned the kettle on. I spooned honey that tasted like the bubble-gum pollen of the kudzu flowers into my mug, proof that even when the rest of the forest doesn't blossom, the bees can find what they need to live.

TRIVIAL PURSUIT

AT THE BOARD GAME COUPLE'S APARTMENT, they ask what you'd like to drink only *after* you've agreed on what game you'll play.

The Board Game Couple often decides the game before you get there, but they make it seem as though you have a say.

The Board Game Couple usually stocks one bottle of red and one bottle of white. A handle of cheap bourbon sits on their bar cart. The husband will bring out four small glasses and a bomber of beer that is usually disgusting for one reason or another—maybe it was fermented with the yeast of one of the brewers' beards or infused with bacon or peppers or chocolate or all three or maybe there are chicken feathers glued to the outside of the bottle for no reason that you can discern. All have been chosen for their novelty and rarity, not for drinkability. You can ask for the wine or the whiskey, but you'll still get a sip from the bomber poured in your glass, and the husband will watch that finger of beer until you make it gone.

At the Board Game Couple's apartment, there is no working doorbell, so you have to call or text them to be let in, but both the husband and wife keep their phones on vibrate and usually leave them in some other room, so be prepared to wait for a while. The Board Game Couple offers to take your coats but then they throw them on a desk chair covered in cat hair. For appetizers the Board Game Couple usually serves popcorn in three bowls, each with a different mix of herbs and spices to give the illusion that they are thoughtful and resourceful about their snacks, not cheap. The hummus is always the new flavor you saw on supersale at the grocery store. The cheese is usually a store-brand block of something mild served with fancy water crackers: creamy nothing on crunchy nothing. You wonder why they choose to splurge on the water crackers over anything else.

For dinner, they serve something out of a slow cooker: chili or pulled pork or a soup, even in the summer months. The wife always realizes, at the last minute, that she's forgotten some key condiment and then spends the rest of the meal asking you if you're sure it's okay, as if you had a choice, as if you might call in an order of takeout to make up for the mediocre bowl before you. The amount of reassurance she requires strikes you as selfish, a greater slight than the missing accoutrement.

The Board Game Couple has only a shitty turntable with old computer speakers to pump the sound through. They won't play music from their phones or an iPod, only scratched, skip-pocked, bargain-bin vinyl. They'll tell you to choose the next record, but that's like telling a prisoner to pick his cell.

The Board Game Couple plays mostly obscure German games with pages of complicated rules. Even if you succeed in convincing them to play a classic—something from Milton Bradley or Parker Brothers—they've always devised some new house rule that they only think to tell you about after you've committed a violation of this rule, and no, you cannot change your move after the fact. If you disagree on the standard instructions, and confirm that your understanding is correct, the Board Game Couple behaves as though they're doing you a big favor by complying. At the start of the game, the husband always complains that he's already so far behind and then you're required to treat him delicately for the next hour or two until it's absolutely clear that he will win—which he always does.

The Board Game Couple mentions they just got back from two weeks in Europe, and you ask them to tell you about it, but they wave you off, insisting that you all focus on the game instead, like you don't really want to hear.

When you tell them about your promotion/your new house/ the birth of your nephew, you get only a single smile from one because the other is busy strategizing his turn.

When you suggest that maybe the next time you hang out, you could go on a picnic or hike, the Board Game Couple talks about the travel Scrabble set they'd bring along.

The Board Game Couple never wants to come to your place. "You don't really have a table big enough to play on, but that's okay. We love to host," the wife says, as if she's comforting you, as if you're worried about putting her out.

Even if it's pouring out when you leave, the Board Game Couple raises their eyebrows when you summon a car to take you home.

As you make your way through the dark side streets, your wife says, "Maybe we don't hang out with them anymore."

You say, "How? What would we do when they ask when we're free?"

"It's not impossible to turn down an invitation," she says. "Say you're overcommitted right now."

"You know he does that thing where he just texts, 'Hey,' so that I'll respond, and then he follows up to ask what we're doing, and if I say, 'Nothing,' then there's no way out."

"So don't respond to that 'Hey' text." Your wife takes out her phone like she wants to stop talking about this.

"Maybe we could find a new couple to play games with," you say.

She looks up, the right side of her face lit with the blue

light of her phone's screen. "Or just to have dinner with?" she suggests.

"Right, that's what I meant," you say. You worry that the driver is judging you and your silly problems, and remain quiet for the rest of the ride.

When the husband emails you an article about the budget cuts for the national parks, you don't respond. You know where such engagement leads.

When he texts, "Big news," you ignore it.

You spend entire suppertimes worrying over your lack of action, but your wife tells you it's no big deal. This is how friendships end. People drift apart and some breakups are more one-sided than others.

You ask the Artist Couple if they want to come over for dinner. You serve Sazeracs and bluefin tuna and home-made tabbouleh. Your wife whips fresh cream and plops it onto the first raspberries of the season.

Dessert bowls emptied, the conversation lulls. "What do we think about playing a game?" you ask.

"Like truth or dare?" The wife sits up in her seat.

"We can't do that again," the husband says. "Someone went a little too far with her dare last time."

"No, no, like Monopoly or Clue." You stand to pull a few options out of the closet.

"I don't think so. We should get going. You have that thing tomorrow," the husband says to the wife.

"Oh yes, right, the thing." Her eyes stay trained on his.

You grab their coats from the bedroom and wait awkwardly while their driver fails to follow his GPS, circling the one-way streets of your neighborhood inefficiently.

"Okay, then, bye for real this time. Don't come back," you wife says, joking, but they sneer like she's serious.

When you lock the door and hear their car pull away, you realize she was serious.

"I don't care if we ever see them again," she says.

"Weren't they better than the Board Game Couple?" you ask.

"Well, they didn't want to play a game, that's for sure." She drains some watery rye from a stray glass.

"Okay, you pick next," you say, as you gather plates.

She smiles. "That's the spirit."

Your wife tells a Childhood Friend to come over, but they make inside jokes that you're incapable of understanding because you weren't there the first time. When the Childhood Friend leaves, your wife says they were just riffing, making everything up, creating new jokes for the next time. "If I'd known that I would have jumped in," you say.

"One potato, two," she says, but you still don't get it.

After dinner with your Gym Friend and his husband, you ask if they'd like to go for a walk, and the husband says he doesn't like to walk after he eats.

"He's afraid of shitting himself," your Gym Friend

says, and laughs, and you can't decide which of your questions to ask and then you've waited too long, and the silence hangs.

Your wife's College Friends bring their baby. It's hard to maintain a conversation with the child distracting everyone.

You invite over your Work Wife and her husband, but all you do is talk about work, and you watch your real wife take her phone out, below table level, to scroll through Instagram, like no one will notice. Maybe no one does.

The Professional Acquaintance your wife met at a conference and his spouse ask if you're interested in a swap even before the salad is brought out. You pretend like it's totally normal that they ask such a thing, surprising yourself by thanking them for the compliment, but declining. At the same time as your wife says, "I have my period," you say, "She's getting over food poisoning." The couple accepts both answers like they are equivalent, and indeed they are: lies constructed to deliver a truth.

Your Neighbors clog the toilet and don't tell you.

Your Fantasy Football League Buddy doesn't apologize when his wife spills red wine on your new taupe couch.

· · ·

Friends of Friends move to your city and call every week to see if you want to get dinner, go to the free show at the park, go for a bike ride. You run out of excuses.

The Woman from Your Wife's Book Group keeps calling you *Kent*.

You stop responding to anyone. You pull the curtains and binge-watch the long list of TV dramas that all of these people have recommended to you. It is summer. You grow pale and bloated. The humidity makes it hard to breathe when you walk to the bus in the morning. This fallow period lasts through fall and winter, and then, when the early mornings turn dark and the late afternoons bright, you slough off the dead skin and take out the recycling.

Your Cousin and his wife come over and you offer jarred salsa and chips that make you ask, *Are these stale?* every time you eat one. Frozen pizza. Domestic beer. They ask to play cards, but you take out a game with tiles and resources, small wooden figures and oddly shaped tokens. Your wife, her hostess skills rickety, hits SHUFFLE on a classic rock album, and your Cousin's wife keeps saying the next song is her favorite and then having to correct herself.

"It's been so long," your Cousin says. "What's new?"

You and your wife can speak only of TV plots.

"We'll have to add those to the list," your Cousin says, generous as always.

Your wife dribbles some beer on her shirt and doesn't even bother with a wet washcloth.

When your Cousin wins the game, you say, "Beginner's luck."

LOITERING

AMY WAS AT THE POINT OF ASKING HERSELF extraordinary questions in earnest. She had lived for a long time projecting a façade of hopefulness, but even that veil had begun to break down. Her friends had taken to asking if she was okay, enough that she suspected they might pose the same question about her to each other in her absence.

Amy sat at a bar among well-to-do industrialists. She could still find little hints of joy in calling modern entities by dated names. She wondered if the men around her could possibly be that successful if they'd chosen to attend such a gathering. If an entrepreneur was stable in their field, did they need the power of a network, of connections? Did they go out in search of such things or did they wait for people to come to them?

Amy had arrived to the bar when it was still empty. The bartender told her she could stay, even though she wasn't supposed to let anyone in without a pass. She let Amy pay for the first drink, but then passed each subsequent cocktail to her, charging her only a wink. "I'm willing to bet these guys can carry one more tab between them all."

Amy stayed long enough that the businessmen cleared out and the bartender didn't tell Amy it was time to go when only the two of them remained in the bar, a busboy having made one final trip to the back and never reemerged.

"It's a bad one, huh?" the bartender asked, and Amy didn't nod because she didn't have to.

"I'm gonna tell you a story. You get tired of listening, you just clear out, no questions asked."

Amy inched her glass to her lips. It was just melted ice now, but she thought maybe that was for the best.

"A friend made a series of bold decisions. I know vague stories are useless, so I'll get specific. She'd die if she knew I was telling you, but she will never know, so here it is.

"Let's call her Peg: a great name. One that never comes up anymore. Peg had just moved to a new city because she'd found a new job. It was a dream sort of job. A job she was unqualified for, but would put more passion and panache into than anyone who had the 'necessary' experience. On her first day, she fell in love with another member of her team, and he seemed just as smitten with her. Her apartment was a steal. She should have been paying triple what she was, but the landlord was old and happy to have a quiet young woman above him. The roof of the building had a pond with three beautiful koi fish in it. After work, she and her young man friend would make dinner together around the immaculate kitchen island. After he did the dishes and she poured them each a glass of wine, they'd go to the roof and watch the fish swim. On the nights they went out, it rained, and on the nights they stayed in, and visited the pond, the weather was clear and perfect."

"Then what?" Amy asked. "She lost it all, right?"

"She married the man. They agreed they both wanted three children and they have birthed three children without issue. They were both promoted in the company, several times. The man took a position at a rival firm and they enjoyed the competition between them. They lived in the apartment until the landlord told them he wanted to sell, and they bought the whole building from him and converted it into a single-family home."

"I hate these people," Amy said, and urged her glass toward the bartender with a single digit.

The bartender poured two more fingers of whiskey into the glass.

"What I'm saying is: Everything worked out. Sure, they had problems from time to time, but don't question the bad, don't question the good. Take what you get and move forward." The bartender threw back a shot of her own.

"That's easy to say when the news is good," Amy said.

"Sure is," the bartender replied. "You drank for free tonight. There's that."

Amy thanked the bartender and pushed back her stool. She went home and when she fell asleep that night, she imagined moving through a tunnel that wasn't only dark, but foggy, too. When she woke up everything was light.

She sent out job applications that day. She texted the woman she'd been too shy to ask out whenever she saw her at the co-op. She walked into the shop she passed on her way to the train, and purchased a wool throw that seemed like what people called an "investment."

Everything went right.

She returned to the bar with her girlfriend.

She went on her own.

She asked the other bartenders when the woman would be working next, but she'd quit. No one knew how to get ahold of her.

On nights when her wife was out of town, Amy would stop in to the bar for an overpriced drink, hoping she might find the bartender to thank her for the way she'd turned nothing into something. One night a woman sat beside Amy. The woman was down on her luck. She'd lost her job, her husband, and with him her house and custody of her kids.

Amy fumbled for something she could say to help the woman and settled for introducing herself. "I'm Amy," she said.

The woman held out her hand. "Peg."

ACKNOWLEDGMENTS

All my thanks to Emily Bell and the rest of the FSG team, including Jackson Howard, Claire Tobin, Naomi Huffman, Chandra Wohleber, Kathleen Cook, and Carrie Hsieh, for making a home where this book can live so happily.

Endless gratitude to Claudia Ballard and my other advocates at WME: Jamie Carr, Matilda Forbes Watson and Alina Flint, Flora Hackett, and Jessie Chasan-Taber.

Many thanks to the editors of the publications in which many of these stories first appeared: Roxane Gay at *The*

Butter, Jonathan Bohr Heinen at *Crazyhorse,* Blake Butler at *Fanzine,* Oliver Zarandi at *Funhouse,* Lincoln Michel of *Tiny Crimes: Very Short Tales of Mystery and Murder,* Meakin Armstrong at *Guernica,* Celeste Ballard and Medaya Ocher at the *Los Angeles Review of Books,* Kim Winternheimer at *The Masters Review,* Justin Daugherty at *New South,* Jodee Stanley at *Ninth Letter,* Alyssa Bluhm at *Paper Darts,* Evan Lavender-Smith at *Puerto del Sol,* the team at the *Southwest Review,* Joel Smith and Drew Burk at Spork Press, and Paul Lisicky at *StoryQuarterly.*

I am indebted to the organizations that have given support to this work, including: the Illinois Arts Council, the Vermont Studio Center, the Virginia Center for the Creative Arts, Hald Hovedgaard: Danish Centre for Writers and Translators, the Oberpfälzer Künstlerhaus, and the Thicket Residency. I'm also thankful to all of the places where I've had the privilege to be employed while these stories were written: Jellyvision, the University of Notre Dame, Illinois Wesleyan University, St. Lawrence University (with special thanks to the Kohlberg Foundation), Northeastern Illinois University, Loyola University, Lake Forest College, StoryStudio Chicago, the Loft Literary Center, and Catapult, among many others, which provided much-needed work that fed both my fiction and my cupboard.

I count myself incredibly lucky to have such a community of supportive friends and family, both writers and not. All of these people feed me in such various and indispensable ways. I am especially grateful to my parents, who never questioned my intentions to pursue any number of foolish endeavors.

Last, but not least, my biggest thank-you goes to my constant champion, Jared Larson.